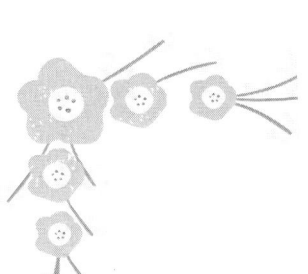

THE
GRUMP
AND THE
GIRL NEXT DOOR

ELLIE HALL

Dedicated to Aurélie, Mary, and Sharon

Hogwash Holler

hôg′wôsh / hol·ler
noun/verb

1. Worthless, false, or ridiculous speech or writing; nonsense
2. To gripe or complain at a high volume
3. A small town that's a little rough around the edges but has a big heart and maybe some secrets too

THE PEST DIGEST

GARDENING & GOSSIP IN HOGWASH HOLLER

BRINGING YOU LOCAL NEWS, DRAMA, AND MORE

Downtown in the once flourishing Hogwash circa 1972

THE WEEKLY STATUS UPDATE BY Y M.E.H.

Could it be the future Mrs. Mechanic? Will she mind getting a little grease under her nails or will she be a big city big shot and not give our resident recluse the time of day?

While the trail may have run cold with Hogan Tickle's famed scavenger hunt, the summer has not. Expect heat, humidity, and more heat because that's how we do it here in Hogwash.

Word on the (Main) Street is the loner mechanic may not be alone much longer. Sources say he wasn't the only one to inherit The Penny Gamble Soda Fountain.

The late proprietor named a second person in her will to co-own the much beloved and now neglected town staple.

Only time will tell, but while you wait, watch, and listen, be sure to send the Pest Digest any scoops—including ice cream.

We sure could beat that aforementioned heat if one (or both) of these partners (in cream) would take some time out from brake jobs and transmission flushes (and whatever it is people do up in Nashville), and wipe the cobwebs off the windows and let a little light in.

However, if the mysterious songstress doesn't make her way down here, that leaves the most eligible bachelor available and I'm not saying I don't call dibs, but I wouldn't object to him revving my engine.

-HOGWASH PEST #1

P.S. Be sure to flip the page for the latest on taming the squash beetles plaguing your summer crops.

Chapter 1

On the Road (Again)

LEXI

I was never a hopeless romantic. More like a hopeful romantic. That is until now.

Also worth noting is that I'm not typically an angry person. I've been told that I'm rather sunny, actually. However, my inner matador waves his red flag, taunting me, daring me to push on the gas pedal.

As I see it, I have two choices.

Drive my car straight into the broad side of the brand new, shiny RAM pickup truck or go south.

The "Beast," as he calls it, belongs to Dirk, captain of the Yahoo Crew. That should've been a warning bell, but I never hear them until it's too late.

I've been at this adulting gig for over ten years now, and somewhere along the way, during my misinformed youth, I thought that on days when I wanted to wear the pink socks with frills, I could wear the pink socks with frills and no one would give me a *look*. You know, the judgy and disapproving one. Or when I craved cookie dough for breakfast, I'd feel just fine by lunchtime.

1

Or, when your lying, cheating, and STEALING ex does you wrong, you could smash into his vehicle like a monster truck at a rodeo.

That would also destroy my classic Plymouth Duster. The thing is on its last legs anyway, but I kind of need it.

This would be the moment for vengeful, savage song lyrics to come to mind. If I had my druthers (not sure what those are, but that was the word that appeared in my brain's vocabulary bank, so we're going with it), T-Swift and I would duet and sing our bleeding hearts out.

It's not a big stretch for that to become a reality. At Club South of Sugar, she bopped in once while I was behind the microphone. Even with the stage lights in my eyes, she glowed with her own aura and not so much as an entourage. Just a friend, as if the two of them casually agreed to go check out some music at a local club on a Tuesday night like normal people.

Never mind the fact that I was the one singing. Nothing ever became of it other than that I was starstruck. Actually, thunderstruck is more like it.

But as I tried to make my way in the biz, the guy I trusted to get me in the door with the music machine moguls betrayed me by giving the song I wrote, "I'd Run into the Storm for You" to my biggest rival, Suzie Lou LeMonde.

If only it were easy to "Shake It Off."

Instead, I drive off, leaving the Nashville nasties in my dust. Dirk can thank me for not totaling his truck. It's not that I'm particularly heartbroken. More like there's a scratch there. But I can't think about that now because I'm nearing my second loop on the city beltway and need to decide where to go. Plus, Dusty, so named because it's a Duster, and Dusty Jones is one of my favorite classic country songwriters, is a gas guzzler.

Having received back the security deposit on my rental—

living two doors down from Dirk would've resulted in arson—I could drive to the airport and catch a flight to Concordia. My friend from college is the Royal Princess of the small, relatively unknown country.

Side note: They have the best chocolate cake in the world. Yes, for real—the part about Penny being a princess and the cake too.

She just added baby number two to the family, and I wouldn't mind meeting that munchkin. My cowboy cousin also lives there with his wife Charlotte and their kids Birdie, Miriella, Johnny, and their newest addition, Wayne.

Do I have baby fever? No. Definitely not. I'd need a husband first, and that's not happening anytime soon. If we'd met two weeks ago, I might be singing a different song. Literally.

Given the fact that mine was stolen and I see no possible recourse, I'll just keep driving.

But where?

A tune ticks vaguely in my mind. Two bars in and I recognize it's Kenny Rogers's "The Gambler" on the radio.

I bite my lip as I near the exit for Interstate 65 South. Squishing up my face because this direction carries an unknown risk, I jerk the wheel and go for it. Don't worry, I didn't cut anyone off in traffic. But I do *whoop* out the window.

"Hogwash-whatever here I come!" I'm home free. Literally. I no longer have a home so I hope things work out, and I don't have to take up car camping.

I'm barely out of Tennessee when the gas gauge breaks off. While stretching my legs and giving Dusty a drink, I call my friend Cleo. She recently opened another location of her shop, Cana Market, in Birmingham.

"Lexi, my country-trotting friend, please tell me you're nearby," she says.

"Probably only a few hours away. How'd you guess?

"Because you only call when you're in town, otherwise, you text. Are you on tour?" Cleo asks.

"I wish that were the case. I'm heading toward Louisiana and passing through."

"Big concert in New Orleans?" Excitement fills her voice.

The opposite weighs mine down. "Nope." I give her the details about Dirk's deception.

"No! That Dirk-bag. I am so sorry. Hang on. Let me go to the other room. It's noisy in here. We're going to pray."

Giving thanks (because let's be real, my situation could be worse) instantly helps me breathe a little bit better.

"So, where are you headed in Louisiana?"

"Hogwash-ootsie. I can't quite remember the second part of the town's name."

"Never heard of it."

"Me neither until a few weeks ago." I tell her about how I was going through a stack of sorely neglected mail. Yes, I'm an adult, but I can't always be bothered with sales circulars and offers for lines of credit because those will only get me into trouble.

I don't have much more than a penny in my purse, but my mother told me not to spend what I don't have.

"I opened an envelope addressed to me in a scrappy scrawl. There was no return info. It contained information about an unexpected inheritance."

"That's incredible. But I am so sorry for your loss. Who should I pray for in your family?"

"Thank you, but fear not, my parents are in fine health. This letter referred to my late pen pal's estate and contained a key."

Cleo lets out a little laugh like I'm joking.

"Are you laughing because I'm a grown woman who had a penfriend?"

"Wait. You're not joking?"

"Not at all. I hadn't heard from Nan in quite a while. The last time I had, her handwriting was shaky and hard to read. I knew she was in her seventies, but she didn't mention anything about a decline in her health. What she did comment on, and with frequency, was her grandson, Cory."

How amazing he was. A perfect gentleman. Handsome, thoughtful, and single.

"Ooh. Sounds romantic."

"I'm on a romance hiatus at the moment, so please don't put in another prayer request."

"Sure. Yeah. Okay," Cleo says breezily.

"Presumably, he sent the letter outlining what was left to me from Nan's estate: The Penny Gamble."

"Like a casino?"

The Kenny Rogers song from earlier comes to mind. "She called it a watering hole, and that's where I'm headed."

"Well, you're welcome to make a pit stop in Birmingham because that's a long ride. Caleb and I bought a property there for when we're in town. When we're not, it's available as a short-term rental. Skybnb, I think we're using. No one is there at the moment, so you're welcome to stay."

"Are you sure?"

"Of course. I wish I was there. Next time, call in advance and I'll drive up."

"Thank you. I'd also like to come down to Blue Bay Beach sometime soon."

"You're always welcome. Oh, and Eisley says hi. She said you should call her."

My mother has commented on how I have friends all over the country—in just about every state because before I put down roots in Nashville, I was on the road with a different ex who wasn't Dirk.

In addition to being a hopeful romantic, I frequently fall fast. Instant love, love at first sight, the kind of person who connects on a deep level quickly.

Well, not today, and definitely not in Hogwash-somewhere or other. I think my days of telling love stories in the form of song are over.

Chapter 2

The First Pancake

LEXI

The next morning, back behind the wheel, I'm barely thirty minutes past Birmingham when the radio dies. I probably need to adjust the antenna, but there's no stopping me now.

In truth, this is symbolic of my life lately and gives me plenty of time to think about how Dirk and Suzie Lou stole my song. They didn't even so much as change a lyric or the tune. No writing credit or so much as an acknowledgment. Running on a sleep and caffeine deficit, I shuffled into my favorite coffee shop and heard my music on the radio. That woke me up fast.

I had a silent but public meltdown because I couldn't believe my ears. It was supposed to be my big hit. A song about slow-burn love and storms that turn into sunsets.

Well, it turns out that love can't be trusted, and neither can I. I've officially given up on dating. From now on, I'm a single lady who will find her own way.

In the last couple of weeks, as I tried to stitch up the pieces of my life and dashed dreams, I developed a nasty case of writer's block. Oh, and that cat scratch on my heart hasn't helped matters.

Looking back, my life has been one long first pancake of the batch. It doesn't quite flip off the pan. More like flops and turns out a little mushy, messy, and is mostly a dud.

My stomach growling, I could go for a pancake right now. Having skipped breakfast, my battery runs low.

When I'm finally halfway across southern Louisiana, a mere fifteen minutes from my destination, I pass through a town called Pouppeville.

I can't help but chuckle. Sounds like Dusty is too. Never mind. That's more of a cranky clank. A sputter and spit kind of sound.

No, no, no.

This is not happening.

From somewhere in the car comes a hiss and a thunk.

This was not part of the plan. Not that I had much of one. This is more of a drive-by-the-seat-of-my-pants operation.

I did not order a breakup and a breakdown—the car. Not me.

Dusty slows to a crawl, giving me enough time to pull off the road before going kaput.

Letting out a huffy breath, I say, "I'm stuck in Pouppeville. Fitting, since my life is in the crapper."

Checking the map, I'm not too far from my destination but not close enough to walk. Having gotten to know Nan, I imagine the Penny Gamble to smell like homemade biscuits and sticky toffee—Nan said she sold candy too. I could go for something sweet right now—gummy bears, red licorice, or even a caramel hard candy. I bet Nan liked those.

However, Mom always said the key to happiness is to keep expectations at rock bottom. Kind of depressing, if you ask me, but that theory hasn't entirely been proven wrong in recent times.

I drop my head to the steering wheel, exhale a long sigh, and then get out to pop the hood. I'm not exactly sure what I'm looking at, but I am certain I shouldn't be seeing so much steam.

Arms folded, I lean on the side of the car. The road runs straight and empty in both directions, with the bayou on one side. I scan the area for alligators and snakes. In a letter, Nan said she had to be careful in her town, so it's safe to assume the same is true here.

As the minutes pass, reality sets in that I'm not stuck on a main thoroughfare, but on the county road that leads to Hogwhatever.

It's high noon and the sun beats down, making the glassy water in the swamp look mighty inviting. I peer through my leopard print Jackie-O glamour sunglasses and consider walking.

Glancing back over my shoulder, when I passed Pouppeville, it was little more than a ghost town. Hogwarts—Harry Potterville would be cool!—is in the other direction. If only I could magic myself there. But I wouldn't dare mess with voodoo or any of that stuff.

I probably shouldn't leave my car either, but I should have paid the extra five dollars for roadside assistance when my car insurance agent suggested the add-on.

Ten, twenty, thirty slow minutes go by, and not a single car passes in either direction. I'm just about out of water. My snacks are gone.

All my worldly belongings (except the boxes stored at my parents' house that they keep reminding me to take) are along for the ride. Is this it? The end of the line?

Then, my ear practically to the ground, I hear a low rumble. I wait, hoping it's a good Samaritan and not a psycho.

You never know.

Throwing caution to the wind, I thrust my thumb out in the universal sign of *I need a ride*. I know it's dangerous, but I'm desperate.

An old loden green Land Cruiser pulls to a stop on the side of the road. The driver reaches across the bench seat and rolls down the window. "Need a ride?"

I lower my sunglasses at this unexpectedly handsome man. I was half expecting a balding guy with a potbelly and buck teeth. This handsome fellow has a full head of brown hair, light scruff peppering a strong jawline, and is bronzed from the southern sun. Chances are he works with hands, given their size and strength. Oh, and his teeth are straight and it looks like he flosses—I wouldn't want him to get gingivitis!

Then my better sensibilities, street smarts, and reality kicks in—I'm alone and this guy could be a felon or want to add to his sunglass collection—people claim the thing they lose most are sunglasses. Those aren't losses, folks. There are thieves—little sunglass burgling house elves robbing us blind.

Lengthening my spine, I say, "I don't know what you're talking about. I wasn't hitchhiking and you can't have my sunglasses."

He frowns. "I didn't say you were...or never mind. Your thumb was out."

Having a level eleven internal freakout, I turn from side to side, realizing how very stranded I am with a stranger—a handsome one, but still. Thinking on my feet, I say, "I was practicing a dance."

"The hood of your car is up." He points to Dusty.

"Yeah, just cooling off. You know." I fan my face. Fine, it serves a dual purpose because it's hot and so is he.

"Where are you headed?" he asks.

"Hogwash-ville, er, burg, um, Hogwash Hampton, maybe?" My face flames with embarrassed nerves.

The guy is probably harmless, but no one other than Cleo knows where I am.

Dad would say this is the height of my irresponsibility. He wouldn't be wrong. Mom would want to know if the driver of the loden green Land Cruiser is available because her daughter —that would be me—is a sweet, southern belle who wandered a little too far down Music Row. They've always appreciated my singing abilities, but mostly in church.

Also, there is no denying the guy in the truck is good-looking in a rough around the edges way. He has eyes that have seen things, but there's a hidden, if not reluctant, softness there too. The kind of person who'd stop and help someone on the side of the road. Give them the shirt off their back. The fanning motion of my hand turns into a flap because my wires are as crossed as Dusty's. I wouldn't object to his T-shirt. Not that I need one. I'm fully clothed and baking from within.

Then a little voice that sniffles from nights spent crying over what Dirk did reminds me I'm off the market.

"Hogwash Holler" The Land Cruiser driver doesn't have a Cajun accent. His voice is more like thunder rolling over hills.

"That's the place," I say with the enthusiasm of a winning game show contestant.

"Headed that way myself. I can bring you there."

His offer is kind, but it could be a ploy to steal the catalytic converter off Dusty...or worse. I size him up and then realize the Plymouth might not have one of those—Mom warned me about it after it happened to Gretchen Bauer when she was visiting the city, but Dad said the Duster is too old to have that kind of exhaust cleaning system.

He inclines his head, awaiting my answer.

Clearing my throat, I say, "Actually, I'll walk. It's a lovely day for a—" In the distance, the sky rumbles. This is bad, dire, a disaster.

"It's another fifteen miles."

"Training for a trek." I pump my arms like I'm speed walking. Like I'm a weirdo.

"You were dancing. Now you're taking a walk? That's your car?" He squints like he's trying to piece together my nonsense story.

"Yep. It runs. Sure. Maybe."

"I can probably fix it."

"That's mighty kind of you, sir. But I'm just stretching my legs." I do some high knees and then reach back to give my quad a nice release.

Lightning strikes in the distance. I startle and grip the door panel of the Land Cruiser.

"Miss, get in." It's a command, but in a sweet kind of way, like he wouldn't want to find me roasted on the side of the road after a lightning storm.

"Is this a hostage situation?" I ask.

"Definitely not. I'm going to Hogwash. I own a service station. You can have your car towed there if you want."

"I'm not sure I should believe you. My bogie sensors aren't going off, but you can never be too sure."

"Bogie?" His sigh is one of long-suffering. "Alright. Suit yourself." He puts the truck in gear and starts to drive off when something he said about owning a service station gels in my mind.

Is this guy Cory, Nan's handsome and single grandson? Actually, forget the last part. Just that he's Cory!

Waving my arms, I holler after him, hoping he'll stop and this isn't some kind of twisted life lesson after I ditched Nashville and my dreams.

Chapter 3

Riding Shotgun

The woman wearing the halter top sundress with sun-
kissed shoulders and glamorous sunglasses that
reveal dark blue eyes hollers something as I pull
away. She waves her arms. Her hair is in a top knot, and it
bobbles as I glance in the rearview mirror.

Once more, I slow to a stop on the side of the road.

She grips the door again. Out of breath, she says, "I'd rather
take my chances with you than with the vultures swooping
down and picking me apart." She references an Alfred Hitch-
cock movie and then shivers.

It's impossible not to inhale her sunflower scent gusting on
the breeze or notice her button nose and chocolate cherry hair.

The woman is a bombshell and a country boy's dream girl
all rolled into one. But that's not why I picked her up. I know
better than to get involved, especially with a woman who was
pacing on the side of the road and then trying to pretend she
wasn't stranded.

Not that I blame her. These roads are relatively quiet, but
occasionally we see city slickers speeding through or back-

woods whack jobs swerving every which way and looking for trouble.

Which I am not.

But I can tell that she is. Trouble, I mean.

She lowers her sunglasses again and gives me a once-over. Her gaze trails from my hands, up my arms—where a few tattoos from my time in the service peek out from my sleeves— and down the length of my body. Her eyes scan my abdomen as if inspecting for anything that could be used as a weapon. Never leave home without one.

However, she's safe with me, even if she thinks otherwise.

Her eyes land on my face as if trying to detect malice or ill intent. "You do this much?"

"What? Pick people up on the side of the road? No, but I wouldn't feel good about leaving you out here. When it gets dark and—"

She waves her hands. "No *ands*. My imagination is plenty vivid. I'm already on edge." She walks away from my restored Land Cruiser.

Well, okeydokey. I put the truck back in gear.

She turns sharply. "Wait. Hold on."

I sigh and return to park. Peaches is going to be annoyed if I take much longer. I don't want to come home and get the cold shoulder. I think about that for a moment before turning to face the unlikely hitchhiker.

"Having second thoughts?" I ask.

"I should get my things. There's no telling how long it'll take for a tow truck to bring Dusty to your shop."

"I take it you're from out of town."

"Nashville." Her smoky, bluesy voice elicits thoughts of lovelorn ballads.

"Then you're not from around here. Passing through?"

She shakes her head. "No and maybe. Not sure yet. Will you wait while I grab my bags?"

I get out and get the bags myself—being a gentleman and all that.

Ten minutes later, I've heard half of her life story and made an important connection. Lexi Dunn is not a stranger. Not exactly.

With a little whimper, she says, "So there you have it. My life was in the gutter, so here I am, leaving a trail of broken hearts and tears in my wake and hoping a fresh start will dry them up."

Dramatic much?

I make a mental note about the heartbreak comment, meaning she is to be avoided. I'm in no shape to venture into relationship territory—I'm broken enough as it is. I tell myself she just rang an alarm bell in case any of the guys in town express interest.

"Oh, and the broken heart and tears were mine," she adds as if that weren't obvious.

"Before, you said hearts, plural."

"Meaning, all the people who won't get to hear my music."

Okay, so she's not a heartbreaker, but she is a bit egotistical. Duly noted.

"I don't mean to say that anyone is worse off not hearing my music. I just meant that people with broken hearts would enjoy it and relate, you know?"

"Yeah, I do," I mutter.

"Music is a great unifier, equalizer, and healer. How many songs have helped me recover from the tatters of unrequited love? Many, many, many."

I agree, but she doesn't leave an opening for me to say so.

"You see, I'm the kind of person who tends to fall fast and hard, which means it also hurts when I fall out of love. Usually, after I learn that the guy is no longer interested." She pauses a bit and goes still.

I don't say a word because this kind of intimate conversation is above my pay grade.

"Oh, wow. I just rambled about all my woes. That was definitely too much information. I backed up my emotional dump truck," she makes a beeping sound, "and unloaded all its contents on a stranger. I am so sorry."

I make a cautious grunt, not necessarily interested in continuing this unsolicited heart-to-heart.

I'm not sure what to make of the presumed Lexi Dunn other than that she's probably nervous. If she's this scatty, it's no wonder she never answered the letters, emails, calls, or text messages I sent. I got tired of trying to reach out and simply sent her the spare key in the last letter, along with some important documents. Given the conversation so far, it's doubtful she read them over carefully.

"Is this what happens when people hitchhike? They just talk nonstop about their lives? I'm not usually like this. I suppose I'm just nervous. Please don't leave me in a ditch somewhere."

"Why would I—?"

Her eyes dart in my direction. "Keep your hands on the wheel where I can see them, mister."

"Keep my hands where you can see them? Are you Deputy Lawson's assistant?" I've been told my humor is drier than the desert.

"Why do you want to know?" She narrows her gaze.

"I haven't done anything to break the law."

"Says every criminal everywhere."

"You were already practically in a ditch, stranded on the side of the road. With the storm sweeping in from the west, trust me, you're better off with me."

"Can I see your license and registration, please?" Lexi asks.

"No, you cannot. How do I know you're not an outlaw?"

"Like Bonnie and Clyde?"

"Is your henchman tailing us?" I ask, glancing in the rearview mirror.

She chuckles. "My henchman? I do not have a Clyde or a Dirk or an anyone." She sighs like she'd invite that kind of reckless love into her life.

"I've heard of a scam where a couple will split up and she'll make it look like she's stranded. Someone who looks wealthy will help, and then the guy will follow them at a distance. When the time is right, the pair will rob the kindly stranger."

"Their romance wasn't all that it was cracked up to be," she says.

"Yeah, I saw the documentary and read Wilson Barrow's book."

"Their story could make for some good songs, though." Her smoky voice verges toward dreamy like she lives halfway in this world and someplace where sound rules.

My gaze cuts to hers for a second because I sensed her looking at me. It seems we've both done our Bonnie and Clyde homework—not that I endorse that kind of criminality. I'm not a police officer. I live on the right side of the law.

Lexi's eyes are the deep blue of dusk. An unfamiliar sensation ripples through me, softening my hard shell. I grip the wheel tighter as the *tick, tick, tick* slows then disappears.

We're both quiet a spell and the commercials on the radio give way to a song about mad love and storms.

In one swift motion, Lexi clicks off the dial. Deep silence fills the cab of the truck.

"Uh, why'd you do that?" I ask, wondering if I'm the one who needs to be concerned about her being a psycho.

"Road trip 101. Whoever rides shotgun controls the radio."

"We're not on a road trip."

And that's the last thing I say for the next ten minutes while she tells me about road trips she's taken all over the country.

"I'm feeling snacky," she says abruptly.

"And chatty," I mutter.

Personally, I prefer silence, except the pregnant kind when I'm with someone who isn't comfortable with even a little bit of quiet.

I flip the radio back on and accidentally toggle the dial to tune to another station. Through a smudge of static comes that same song.

Over the music, she says, "I could really go for a snack. Is there a convenience store or market in Hogwash whatchamacallit?" Before I answer, she turns down the radio and says, "I didn't hear what you said."

Either she's been on the road too long and wants to chat, prefers the sound of her own voice, or the song, *I'd Run into the Storm for You* did something to offend her.

Chapter 4

A Bag of Bad Ideas

With only five miles to go, the crackling in the clouded sky catches up with us, and I have to slow to a crawl. If I were in my regular truck I'd haul on through, but this is a fully restored 1973 Land Cruiser, and any classic car owner worth their weight in steel and fiberglass knows to take it easy. Wouldn't want all my hard work to end up in a heap on the side of the road.

We pass the sign that says, *Welcome to Hogwash Holler Township. Established, 1925.*

"Hogwash Holler," Lexi says in her smoky voice. "Who'd have ever thought I'd end up here? If you're wondering, I was an aspiring songwriter and singer, trying to make my way up in Nashville. Two years ago, a fan sent me a sweet note, old-fashioned style, on stationery. Reminding me of my grandmother. I recently learned she passed away and left me her shop…" She trails off as if trying to keep the story and her sadness separate.

Ding, ding, ding.

This new piece of information confirms that the hitchhiker

is none other than the Lexi Dunn whom I've been trying to contact for well over a month. But that doesn't mean I trust her.

"Did you know her or where her shop is?"

"Hogwash Holler is a small town," I answer vaguely because a salty thought comes to mind.

"What a funny name. I could never remember the second part. Are you from Hogwash Holler?"

"Nope." I leave it at that because I don't want to discuss the circumstances that brought me here.

The windshield wipers squeak on the glass as they clear the rain. Lexi looks around at the rough-around-the-edges town. You could collect enough peeling paint to fill a swimming pool —there's an empty one at the community center—and every day there are new cracks in the cement. Chipped shingles flap in the breeze. The weeds growing on the sidewalk don't get out of the way when the rare pedestrian strolls by.

"It's not much to look at, but believe it or not, it was once a thriving town—a hub in this area. Time and greed left it to ruin."

"It's not exactly what I expected. Nan described it more as—"

"As she remembered in its heyday?" I guess.

"Yeah. I'd say so."

I pull in front of the old soda fountain and come to a stop.

"I kind of expected a hip, trendy joint given the name The Penny Gamble," Lexi singsongs.

"Not what you were expecting," I repeat. She's certainly not what I was expecting, but I keep my identity to myself. During the ride here, I learned enough about her to have the sense to avoid getting involved in her drama.

The rain slows, and Lexi lowers from the truck, not minding the fine mist in the air. "Nanette Peterson, just what did you have in mind?" she whispers, glancing from the Penny Gamble storefront to me as if I'm her last tie to her life before she entered the town limits. As if I have the answers. I might.

I spotted the shoebox full of letters they exchanged but didn't want to read the content. That would've been intrusive. "I imagined Nan's pen pal to be closer to her in age."

Lexi tilts her head and sharpens her gaze. "I didn't mention that we were pen pals. How'd you know about that?"

"I've been the one trying to reach you. Letters, emails, texts."

"That was you? I thought it was a spam text, soliciting my social security number or trying to get my bank card pin." She winces. "I blocked you."

I start to answer her question to explain who I am but stop short. Instead, I keep my walls up. "Yet you found your way here."

As if remembering her manners, she says, "Sure did with thanks to you. By the way, I'm Lexi Dunn." She extends her hand for me to shake.

It would be rude if I didn't take it. A spark tries to light between our palms, but I'm thankful the moisture from the rain lets it fizzle.

I say, "And I'm running late."

Her full lips slide into a faint frown. "Oh, well, thanks again. I guess I'll just find my way into that haunted building. Considering I survived hitchhiking, it would seem good fortune favors me today. Hopefully, I didn't exhaust the supply." She grips her bags in both hands.

Instead of the storm driving away the summer humidity, the air balloons with the kind of stickiness I'll never get used to, even though I was born and raised not far from here on the other side of the Louisiana-Texas border. Must've been the long swaths of time I spent in the desert and mountains. Then again, I'd never quite acclimatized to those regions either.

And I'll definitely not get used to Lexi next door, even if she only lasts one day in Hogwash.

The sun peeks out from behind the clouds at the same time Molly Hazelwood and Roxanne Lagniappe, the town's busybodies, march down the street. Here for less than five minutes and they already caught a whiff of the newcomer.

My stony, quiet nature kept the neighborhood welcome wagon at a relative distance. Though, I imagine these three will blab all afternoon, during which Molly and Roxanne will try to get some dirt on me from Lexi, not that I gave her any.

Molly is the shorter, rounder, and generally more talkative of the pair—the ringleader. Roxanne is the taller, thinner, and quieter of the two women—though she's always snapping a piece of gum. It recently came to my attention that they both have a crush on me. To my surprise, Roxanne made the move first. Hopefully, I let her down easily.

In a low voice, I say, "Careful what you say and do. The people here have long necks."

Lexi tucks her chin back and her eyes widen as if she's afraid there's something in the water. "Like giraffes?"

"The kind of people who crane their heads to listen to everyone else's business, not minding their own."

"Does that mean they like to gossip?"

"They have a weekly publication that started as the Pest Digest, a gardening journal turned local rag when Molly Hazelwood wanted revenge on Albert Woodbury for dressing up her chicken for Halloween."

"Sounds scandalous."

"Quite."

"Does that include you? Any skeletons in your closet?" Lexi waggles her eyebrows.

"A few." I give a short shake of my head. "But if you're asking if I engage in the airing of other people's dirty laundry? Not a chance."

"You seem like the kind of guy who sticks to yourself."

She all but says I'm a recluse. Lately, she wouldn't be entirely wrong. At that, it's time to bid Lexi Dunn *adieu* so I don't invite any trouble into my life. Had enough of that.

"Thanks for the ride." She hesitates. "See you around."

With a nod, I put the Land Cruiser in drive, but I don't go far and pull into Cory's Automotive Service Station right next to the Penny Gamble. We even share a fence.

In the rearview mirror, I watch as Molly and Roxanne approach. Instead of stopping, they do a quick pass. Probably an assessment before they descend. Lexi had it right about the vultures, except they're here in Hogwash, not out on the county road.

She gives the two women a slight smile of acknowledgment but mostly focuses on the sign in front of my best friend's service station as if trying to puzzle something out.

When I round to the back, where I live in a cottage built in the expansive area behind the shop, Peaches gives me a long side-eye, which I deserve. I was gone longer than I expected. But then, as if she can't help herself, the corgi runs a little askew in my direction before bounding into my arms, nearly knocking me over. Of course, I crouch to scoop her up. Unable to contain her wiggles, she licks my face like a madwoman.

"Who missed me? I missed you, girl, I sure did."

Yes, I baby-talk my dog. Don't judge. She's the only light in my life and because she doesn't know about my past, she doesn't shun me, unless I stay away too long and miss her afternoon treat.

"We're having burgers for dinner, girl. I'll let you take a nibble."

Later that night, as I drowse in bed, I recap the surprising encounter with Lexi. She's probably here to cash her check and then she'll try to sell the Penny Gamble.

Not on my watch.

This whole thing is a bag of bad ideas. I cannot fathom what Nan was thinking, leaving equal shares of her soda fountain shop to the two of us. But I'll do my best to ignore Lexi and this situation for as long as possible. Then again, I know all too well that burying my head in the sand doesn't make my problems go away. No, they just slowly chafe at me until callouses form.

Ignoring her won't be easy—not with those blue eyes that see everything or that voice that is like a song I didn't realize that I'd forgotten.

When I stopped on the side of the road, I'd said I was heading to Hogwash Holler, which was true, but occasionally when I leave town, I feel the pull to move north, away from the past, where no one knows me.

Cory and I once went skiing in a little town in Montana called Hawk Ridge Hollow. They had the best pizza and pie shop called *Costa's Pizza and Pie*. An unusual combination, yes, but it worked. The town was the kind of place Hogwash dreams it could be with a bustling Main Street, thriving businesses, and not a piece of litter in sight.

As a rule, I stay away from cities, but Hogwash has seen better days and could use a makeover.

With the summer breeze whispering through my window, to my surprise, for once, I'm content here. Maybe it's my backyard oasis, Peaches, or something else altogether.

As usual, in the background, the country music CD Nan gave me plays. I've been listening to it to help me fall asleep since I turned up in town—and punishing myself because I wasn't a better friend to Cory.

The songs on the CD don't knock me out because they're boring. Not at all. The woman's voice is like a smoky, velvety lullaby, and soon I'm out cold.

Chapter 5

Meet Rude

LEXI

It's hard to get Cory's voice out of my head with the way he sweet-talked his sweetheart when he got home.

It's not that I was being nosy. Not even a long-necked neighbor. Rather, it wasn't easy to ignore him on the other side of the fence.

After he dropped me off, he pulled into Cory's Automotive Service Station, which is right next door to the Penny Gamble Soda Fountain.

Turns out the guy who picked me up in his classic Land Cruiser, wearing duck utility work pants made of canvas or some other stiff fabric, and a blue button-down mechanic's shirt is none other than Nan's grandson, Cory.

In every letter she wrote, she tried to play matchmaker, telling me how great he was—how considerate, thoughtful, and generous. Oh, and romantic.

But I'm no longer a hopeful or hopeless romantic, for that matter. I'm a nothing romantic. As in, that word is no longer part of my vocabulary and I don't want a thing to do with it.

That probably won't be hard here in Hogwash if I decide to stay awhile, which is up for debate. But dating Cory is not.

Sorry, Nan. The guy has the manners of a potato. And it's no wonder he's single. Cory has the personality of a thornbush.

He has the intense and intimidating look of an action movie hero and the eyes of a romcom heartthrob. And okay, fine, his lips are nice to look at. Lush. So very lush. Under his scowl, there is a handsome face with a strong jaw and a nice mouth. Have I mentioned that?

Also, I don't want anyone, especially my parents, to worry. I wouldn't have gotten in the truck with him had I not looked into his eyes. You can tell everything about a person by their eyes. His are dark brown. Despite every other broody and slightly dangerous aspect of him—what with the tattoos peeking out from the wrist of his shirt—his eyes are kind.

But he is not.

Moving on and moving in.

Crazy that it was him who sent me the key to Nan's apartment behind the soda fountain shop. It's a single level, and the door has a window with lacy curtains—exactly what I'd expect from Nan.

Stepping inside, on the right, the efficiency opens to a postage stamp-sized living room and to the left, a galley kitchen with enough room for two people to pass each other if they sidestep in a parallel fashion. I've worked in food service and it would necessitate a courtesy, *Behind you*, when passing.

Off the main space is a small bathroom with a Pepto Bismol pink bathtub and white subway tile. The bedroom also boasts lacy curtains and a full-size brass bed with what looks like a handmade quilt. The place is as neat as a pin.

It's cozy like a hug from a grandma and I adore it.

"Thanks, Nan," I whisper, wondering about her life beyond what she shared in her letters.

She never married and worked tirelessly—ever grateful to her loyal customers who were like her family, along with Cory, of course.

But there aren't any photographs or personal touches in the small house, er, apartment since it's not freestanding. Perhaps he took them when he learned she left the place to me.

Taking another spin around the space, I open drawers and cabinets. There's a small collection of cleaning products and exactly four items of each type of dishware you'd need: plates, bowls, and silverware. Plus, cooking staples like a pot, a pan, a spatula, and an assortment of baking trays. I exhale, content enough to call this home. At least for tonight.

Before it gets too late, I want to know what I'm dealing with business-wise, so I scoot to the front of the building.

When Cory dropped me off, two women passed on the sidewalk in front of the Penny Gamble. I gave them a friendly smile, but they were deep in conversation and hardly looked my way.

If I were Tay Tay, they would've stopped, dropped, and asked for a selfie. Alas, my career didn't reach that zenith. It never even left this atmosphere, never mind the Nashville bubble.

Hogwash Holler must turn in early because it's quiet on the street. Across the way is a beauty parlor and the post office. Several more buildings run along the no-stop light town.

The brick exterior of the Penny Gamble needs paint. It's on the corner of Main Street and Metairie Road. The lower half is light turquoise and the white upper section backs a copper sign with the words *The Penny Gamble*. I imagine it was quite eye-catching in its day. The door is on the corner and recessed with a pair of planters filled with dead weeds on either side. Two large windows flank the entrance with benches that have broken slats beneath them and more planter boxes, hosting more dead flowers.

Peering through the glass, my stomach feels like a hose with a kink, but it's not only because I'm hungry. This place is spooky.

From the other side of the fence, the scent of grilled burgers wafts invitingly. I highly doubt Cory will be a welcoming neighbor and invite me over.

I'm not sure the electricity at the soda fountain is on—and let's be real, it has an abandoned, haunted vibe. From the front, it looks like swamp ghosts use the place to party and it's getting late. Tomorrow, during daylight hours, I'll venture inside.

I've taken enough risks for one day.

Later that night, when I get into bed, my thoughts fill with swamp ghosts. Are they real or did my overactive imagination conjure the concept? I don't know, but the strange noises and whistling from the apartment don't convince me they're the stuff of myths and legends.

I can't sleep, so I browse social media on my phone. The connection is lousy and the pages load slowly, which is probably just as well because everyone in the country music sphere is blowing up about Suzie Lou's song, aka my song. The one I wrote the lyrics and music to.

The problem is, I never recorded a demo and hardly wrote down the words. The only thing I can figure out is that when I showed up at Dirk's, unable to contain my excitement, he used his phone to record me singing. I knew I'd written my hit. Not that I aimed to be a one-hit wonder, but with some songs you just know.

Instead of wallowing in misery, I text my friend Everly. She lives on an island in Michigan with a veritable Viking who is the love of her life and a former NFL star. They're used to small-town life, er, no town since they're the only house for miles and leagues. I tell her briefly about the soda fountain and where I am.

Everly: Never heard of the place.

Me: You'd be hard-pressed to find it on a map. I could go for some retail therapy, but I think the only game in town is a feed and seed store.

Everly: That bad?

Me: Worse. I'm pretty sure the soda fountain is haunted.

Everly: I'll send you my cookie dough recipe. It's magic.

Me: Please and thank you. I miss you, friend.

Everly: Me too! You can come visit anytime. Seriously. These kids love their Auntie Lexi. In the meantime, do you know anyone there?

Me: Just a big meanie.

The little dots indicating she's writing blink for a long moment as I think about Cory. His deep voice with a Texas accent is like thunder rolling over country hills. Ooh, that could be a song lyric. Then I remind myself that I am no longer writing music. I am no longer a singer or songwriter. I am nothing. Well, except for the owner of a soda fountain. Whatever that is. I'm still not entirely sure.

Everly: Sorry, a kid needed a water refill. This is the fourth time he's come out with a request. We've hit the bedtime battle years. Anyway, what were we talking about? Oh, yeah, your super-hot meanie.

Me: I didn't say he's super-hot.

Everly: You called him a meanie.

Me: Exactly.

Everly: What does he look like?

Me: Dark brown eyes. Dark brown hair. Five o'clock shadow. Lips.

I press send and then realize I added that last part, implying that Everly is right. But just like my nonexistent music career, I am not looking for a handsome but broody man and dreaming about a happily ever after or available to date. My love life is in the gutter on Ashville Ave in Nashville. Scrambling before Everly can call me out, I reply.

Me: I mean, he has lips as an anatomical feature. I am not thinking about his lips. We did not have a meet cute.

Everly: But he's cute, right?

Me: More like rude. It was a meet rude.

The dots blink for a few minutes, and I imagine Everly is busy with her kids. I'm about to close my eyes when she sends an apology, along with a link to a show on HLTV called Designed to Last. She said it's her guilty pleasure when she can't find refuge in retail therapy or cookie dough. She promises that she'll email the recipe.

I could go for cookies right now. But it's late and the cupboards are bare. Instead of the smell of chocolate, my thoughts drift to the guy who smelled faintly like engine grease mixed with the manly scent of clove and spice...my new next door neighbor.

Chapter 6

Swamp Zombies

LEXI

I survive the night without getting haunted, so that's a plus.

On the negative side, the steady patter of rain tells me that the storm from yesterday had a little brother. Also, if the clock on the bedside table is correct, I overslept, not that I had a wake-up call. However, it's my first day. I don't want to give the long-necked neighbors the impression that I'm lazy.

Everything is always less spooky in the sunshine, but I have to see what I'm dealing with at the soda fountain despite the gloomy weather.

After a shower and pulling on cut-off shorts and a tank top, I scoot outside and am about to round to the front of the building when I notice a short, covered path that leads to a rear door. I take it to avoid a second shower of the day.

Sliding the key in the lock, it doesn't click, meaning it was open. Maybe people have been partying in the vacant space.

When I pull open the door, the hinges creak loudly like a ship in the movies right before it goes down. It's an undeniably haunting sound. The cobwebs and slightly stale air don't help either.

The dim light of the day provides enough for me to find a light switch. A bare overhead bulb flickers to life, illuminating a short hallway with a couple of doors on either side. At the end is another that must open to the soda fountain's main room.

The door on the right has an old-timey lacquered wooden plaque that says, *Nan's Office.* Underneath, someone tacked a message that says, *Only knock if you have good news. Come right in if it's bad and you need to talk.* The word, *Bathroom* is painted on the second door. The last door has a little, hand-lettered sign that says, *Leave a smile, laughter, and love when you come and when you go.*

That's a good sign. Literally.

Exhaling, I turn the knob. However, I can't muster any of the above. No smiles, laughter, or love.

Unlike Nan's apartment, the soda fountain is a neglected wreck. Like the ship heaved on the waves and sent everything from side to side repeatedly. Tables are askew, chairs toppled, and every surface has a thick layer of dust, not to mention old rags, discarded boxes, and debris scattered everywhere.

The swamp ghosts hit the iceberg and took the Titanic down. My stomach sinks.

An old-fashioned jukebox sits against a brick wall. The rest are plaster or batten board. The top of the massive music player forms a bubbled arch. In the center is a pink pig with white wings. I imagine when plugged in, that part lights up. Scuffs on the wooden base and a crack in the glass on the front make me wonder if it would even work.

I've seen a few jukeboxes at joints in Nashville, but nothing like this with its tubes and chunky buttons. If nothing else, I'd like to clean it up and give it a whirl.

This whole place is a relic, a step back in time and a record of its passage in the form of grime, grease, and dust.

Just then, a rapping sound comes from the front of the building. I startle and let out a sharp breath. I put my hands where I can see them.

"I come in peace," I say before realizing someone knocked.

I part the slats to the window blind on the door, but the glass is smudged. The bolt sticks and the handle is sticky.

I expect the police, prepared to arrest me for suspicious activity, or a friendly neighbor to invite me over for sweet tea. We'd get to chatting and they'd explain the soda fountain's state of neglect.

Instead, Cory stands under the overhang, protected from the rain. The grump from next door does not appear to come in peace. Dressed in his mechanic's uniform, he wears a scowl.

"Good morning," I say, following the directive on Nan's sign.

He hands me a manila envelope. "Thought you'd want to have these."

"Guess you don't adhere to Nan's reminder to 'Leave a smile, laughter, and love when you come and when you go,'" I murmur.

Hands on hips, Cory surveys the space and his expression flashes with something impossible to identify. He hides his emotions under a mask that's part smug and part salty like he's mad at the world or himself—I can't be sure.

"You'll be happy to know that I survived last night. The apartment was nice and tidy," I say, trying to let in some sunshine or poke him in the ribs. I'm not clear on that either.

"That's how Nan liked things. I made sure she stayed comfortable."

My stomach growls. "Not much in the pantry, but thankfully I had some soup cracker packets in my purse. Yep, been living on Saltines and rest stop condiments for two days."

Cory narrows his gaze like that's not his problem. "The welcome wagon hasn't come by yet?"

I give my head a slow shake, not sure what that is.

"I'll start working on your car this morning, get you out of here before you get too bored."

"Who said I'm leaving?" It's not like I have anywhere else to go.

He looks around the room and grunts again as if the answer is right in front of my face. He wouldn't be wrong. The place is enough to chase the Designed to Last team out of town.

"I haven't decided yet. Granted, this place isn't turnkey, but..." I walk in a small circle, taking in all the work that would be required to make even the most loyal customers have the slightest of appetites.

Behind the marble counter, bordered by chrome spinning stools topped with cracked turquoise vinyl, are mirrors and more subway tile backing a bank of vintage soda glasses, complete with the soda fountain itself and all the flavor dispensers. I'm afraid to open the cooler in case it contains moldy ice cream or a fat raccoon.

The retro white and black checkered floor could use a solid buffing, but it's classic in its way. Then there is the tin ceiling where I have no doubt spiders the size of doughnuts make their home.

"Oh! Maybe we could serve doughnuts too." Giving my head a shake, I say, "Hold up. I am getting way ahead of myself. But inspiration sparks and that's more than I can say for my musical life at present." I mutter that last part because dashed dreams are depressing even when they're not your own.

Like moving through an obstacle course, I carefully pick my way past the discarded furniture and toward the far wall where candy displays feature prominently. I poke through some boxes and find one labeled *The Queen's Jewels*. "Think I found the motherload."

Cory grunts. Yep, he's still here, whether watching to make sure I don't injure myself and contract tetanus or destroy something—I doubt the liability insurance is current. Then again, I'm not sure how I could make his beloved grandmother's soda fountain worse unless I had a flame thrower. The swamp ghosts did the job for me.

I rifle through the box and remove packages of candy. "Eureka! Treasure!"

"Figures, you'd be here for the payday."

"Huh?" I'm about to ask what he's talking about when I plug my mouth with a ring pop. Sweet, sweet sugar.

I forgot this place offered soda, ice cream, and candy too. The chalkboard menu is indecipherable, but I recall Nan mentioning Cory's favorite soda was the banana and chocolate-peanut butter candy fizz, which sounds like a combination of all three.

"You're eating the treasure?" Either Cory has the driest sense of humor ever, which is to say none at all, or he's serious.

I pop the ring out of my mouth. "It's candy."

"It's probably old."

Such a grouch.

"Candy doesn't go bad. It's made of sugar and chemicals. Plus, the package was sealed."

"Candy for breakfast? Chemicals?"

I check my watch. "It's brunch. And someone didn't invite me over for burgers, so I'm hungry."

He huffs and scrubs his hand down his face, stopping at the scruff along his jaw as if he *can't* with me.

I cross the room, taking in the space, and not Cory. Nope, definitely not looking at him. It wouldn't kill the guy to smile or use words instead of the little *Hhh* sound that repeatedly comes from his throat. It's kind of like a ponderous grunt, but far be it from me to try to decipher his gloomy lips, I mean language. I am not thinking about the man's lips.

"Under the grime and grunting, there is potential. Probably."

"Hhh." There he goes, making that sound again.

"Grunting? Really?"

He flashes me a sharp look.

My cheeks warm as I realize that I said that out loud. To cover my tracks, I say, "Sheesh. This building sure grunts and groans. It could be haunted. Do you know much about swamp ghosts?"

"It's definitely not haunted."

"How do you know?"

Cory casts his gaze upward as if making a plea for patience.

"What about swamp zombies?"

With a shake of his head, he casts me a look like he's not going to waste his breath trying to convince me they're not real either.

Giving the manila envelope a little shake, I say, "So is this an instruction manual?"

"No, they're the letters you wrote to Nan."

I cringe and the blush across my cheeks deepens. I treated my letters to Nan like a diary, sharing all my love life and lovelorn secrets. Granted, I never named names, but if Cory read them, he'll know how I've had my heart stepped on, torn up, and tossed in the sewer. I don't have a good track record when it comes to choosing guys.

As if reading my mind, or my body language, which sends the flush all over because that would mean he's looking at me, Cory says, "If you're wondering if I read your letters, I did not."

"Thank you for respecting my privacy."

"And if you're wondering what Nan would've wanted you to do with that check—"

"What check?"

"The one with the copy of her will, the deed, and everything I sent with the key."

I'm quiet for a beat.

Cory cocks his head. "You didn't read it did you?"

Biting my lip, I give mine an innocent little shake.

"Did you read the letter I wrote?"

"Not carefully. When I finally opened it, I had a lot going on in my life." Letting out an exhale, I add, "Like a lot, and I—"

He turns to leave, and it's hard to ignore how he both walks with purpose and saunters. It seems like an impossible thing. Something to write into a song. No, nope. Not going even to think about my dead daydream song-making machine.

"Okay then, buh-bye," I say as the door whisks shut behind him. "Cory does not live up to Nan's praise of her grandson. He's Mr. Bad Manners."

But my mother always said to, *Kill 'em with kindness.* I don't intend to take any casualties, and I love Everly's cookie dough, but I have my own secret weapon and it involves a cast iron pan. Don't worry, I won't hit him over the head with it, though I won't lie, it occurred to me.

Nope, Cory is going to change his tune when he sinks his teeth into The Original Lexi Dunn Sm'ookie.

Chapter 7

Soda Jerk

I 'm halfway under the body of a late 90s pickup when I hear Molly Hazelwood's high-pitched childlike voice. I instantly stiffen, afraid she's here at the shop.

Listening carefully, and willing to roll the rest of the way under this vehicle and hide here all day if I have to—I try to avoid her and Roxanne, her sidekick, at all costs. A pair of busybodies, I was the talk of the town when I arrived in Hogwash, fresh off the boat—a naval warship in the Indian Ocean.

Technically, I had a desk job after taking a bullet hole or two. Okay, three. Ahem, five. Had it happened ten years ago, I probably would've lost my leg. Thank goodness for tourniquets and modern medical technology.

Like my best friend and I talked about for our retirement plans while we served our country, now, I just want to restore old vehicles, listen to country music, and avoid mosquitos.

And the writers of the Pest Digest.

Also women, specifically Lexi Dunn.

She's too chaotic, scattered, and dreamy. I mean, like her head is in the clouds. I don't mean how her long lashes brush her cheeks when she closes them to think—possibly envisioning what the Penny Gamble used to look like.

A couple of days ago, it was hard not to watch her glide around the neglected soda fountain, a sunny contrast to the cloudy day. I definitely don't wonder how soft her chocolate cherry hair must be to touch or what her full lips would be like to—never mind.

I'm too broken for a relationship, especially with the girl next door who is as sweet as pie. I could really go for a slice from *Costa's*...pizza too. I should fire up the brick oven in the backyard soon.

But the bottom line is that I have too many scars inside and out, meaning, it'll just be Peaches and me around these parts.

Speaking of parts, I need to put in an order for Lexi's Duster. I go to the shop office and flip on the computer. As usual, it flashes as though having a fit. The old thing fights with itself regularly about whether to turn on or not. Instead, I flip through the old, thick catalog searching for a reference number, so I can put in a call for the replacement pump old school style.

Peaches whines to be let out. We head to the side door adjacent to the yard where my dog and I have our little oasis. Cory's father was smart when he bought this property because he purchased the acre behind it as well. I imagine he had plans for a scrapyard, but I made better use of it.

Molly and Roxanne's voices rise and fall from the other side of the stockade fence as they tell Lexi they're the Hogwash welcome wagon.

"I haven't decided whether or not I'm going to stay or go," she says.

Go, go, go.

Then a strange thing happens, a voice that sounds suspiciously like Cory's whispers in my mind, telling me not to be such a pigheaded jerk.

I'm about to check my head when I realize it's probably because Lexi said Cory's name. She comments on how her car is over here and in need of repairs.

"Well, it's in good hands," Molly says.

"Very good, strong, capable hands," Roxanne adds breathily.

"He had a lot of grease under his nails," Lexi says as if trying to talk herself out of something.

"I notice yours are such a pretty shade of lilac. I work at Hogwash Hairwash & Style. We also do facials, manis, pedis, and special occasion updos. If you ever want yours done, I'm your gal. Well, the receptionist, but I can get you an appointment." Then Molly whispers something, probably about not being licensed, not that people in Hogwash pay much attention to bureaucracy and red tape.

"Us Hoggers do things our way." Roxanne snaps her gum.

I clap lightly for my dog to come inside, but Peaches found something mighty interesting to sniff next to the fence.

"Anything else I should know about this town?" Lexi asks.

"Well, there is the crocogator," Molly says in a hush.

I force myself not to chuckle because that's the stuff of urban, or rather, rural legends—same as swamp ghosts and swamp zombies.

"Do you mean an alligator?" Lexi asks.

"No, a crocogator."

"Like a crocodile?"

"While some people think alligators and crocodiles are the same, there are some key differences," Roxanne says with authority.

Lexi says, "We don't have either of those in Tennessee."

Roxanne goes on, "I reckon not. Crocs' and gators' snouts are distinctly different along with their teeth and the color of their hide."

"I've never seen one in real life." Trepidation fills Lexi's voice as if this information leaves her more scared than prepared.

"It's also worth noting that you usually find alligators in fresh water. Crocodiles prefer saltwater," Roxanne continues.

"There are exceptions," Molly says.

"And of course, crocs are generally more aggressive."

"What about the crocogator?" Abject fear laces Lexi's voice.

"It's a hybrid, and the deadliest of them all," Roxanne says.

"Also it's an albino."

"So not a greenish alligator, er, crocodile. I mean crocogator? Is it a ghost?" Lexi says.

I can imagine the two women nodding with grave warning. I recall Cory telling me tales about the supposed albino hybrid that haunted the bayou.

Lexi asks, "Have you ever come across it?"

Molly and Roxanne start bickering about the last crocogator sighting.

"If he comes knocking on the door to the Penny Gamble, I'll be sure to tell him to get lost." Lexi's laugh is a little shaky.

I can't help but find it endearing—not that she's genuinely scared. More so that she doesn't have anything to worry about. The crocogator isn't real. Though I guess it helps that nothing scares me, not even bullets.

"So you're going to fix it up?" Molly asks, having an opening to collect the dirt she loves so much.

"Status pending. There's a lot to consider. I spent yesterday taking inventory and researching what it would mean to run a place like this."

"Well, Nan just unlocked the door and started serving."

"That easy, huh?" Trepidation fills Lexi's voice.

Peaches stares at the fence with her little doggy eyebrows

pinched together like she feels left out. Poor thing seems to think if she looks at the wooden slats long enough, a doorway will open and she'll be able to pass through and hang out with the ladies. It's also very likely the Hogwash welcome wagon brought the gravy train, as in biscuits and an assortment of other food items. When they finally caught up with me, they gave me enough food to feed a SEAL Platoon.

I don't want to call Peaches inside in case Lexi, Molly, and Roxanne hear me. I have work to do and Pest Digest content collectors to avoid.

And I've been successfully avoiding Lexi for the last couple of days. Well, I've been trying to avoid her.

As if she can read my mind, or wants to join the social hour next door, Peaches barks.

"Shh," I hiss.

There's a reason I've been avoiding Lexi and it's not only because seeing her, hearing her, and talking to her causes something strange to tick inside—it's the kind of thing that would cause a car owner to bring in their vehicle for a diagnosis.

Lexi waved at me the other day. I didn't do the neighborly thing and wave back. Why? There went that ticking and I'm the only mechanic in town—that would be like suggesting a doctor perform their own surgical procedure, at least the minor outpatient kind.

The next afternoon, she cruised over to check on her car. The thing is in rough shape. Turns out she hadn't had it serviced in over a year. She's lucky the engine didn't blow because boy, was she thirsty. And just because she's pretty I can't put her ahead of the other jobs—the Duster, not Lexi.

There goes that tick again.

That doesn't mean she can jump the line. Bruce Landry's Buick Century needs a brake job and Missy Groveland asked me to check a squeak on her Corolla. Like everyone else, Lexi has to wait her turn.

Anyway, I won't accept payment if it comes from the small fortune Nan left both of us. That's for the Penny Gamble. Given that big, round number, I expect Lexi to skip town as soon as the Duster runs, leaving me to fix up the soda fountain myself. When I get around to it.

The only thing Lexi and I have in common is that Nan left the shop to *us*. If I'm smart, I ought to get rid of her real quick—if the crocogator tall tale doesn't do the job for me. Actually, I'm surprised she's lasted this long. Hogwash is a far cry from Nashville.

Peaches barks a few more times and then whines when I gesture that she come inside. Who's the long-necked neighbor now, listening in on the ladies' chatter?

That would be my dog and me.

Lexi's smoky voice is like a magnet, luring me to listen a little longer. Because Peaches refuses to budge and come inside, I slam the mental door on that idea...and the one behind it, suggesting I find something we have in common. Nope. That's not happening.

Lexi is a big-city girl with fancy nails. Meanwhile, I have grease underneath mine.

There is sunshine on her side of the fence. I have full cloud cover over here.

From what she said, her heart is looking, longing for love. Mine is locked up behind bars where it belongs.

The thing is, if I can't save a friend, I don't deserve to protect and honor a woman.

And she managed to ignore the letter I sent along with the emails, calls, and texts—I found Lexi's contact info among Nan's things.

The worst part is she didn't even come to the funeral. All of

Hogwash turned out. That tells me, likely, Lexi is just in it for the money. Then again, it had been about a year since she and Nan corresponded.

Which, if I'm being fair, makes sense, given the timeline of Nan's cognitive decline. But that's not something I want to think about.

However, it's hard to avoid thoughts of Lexi or ignore her smoky voice, floating over the fence. It's like a song that's stuck in my head, urging me to linger. She comments on the soda fountain.

Then Molly says, "It used to be that people would gather at the Sunrise Café in the morning, head to the Laughing Gator Grille for lunch, then pop into the soda fountain for an afternoon refreshment."

"Or after dinner, they'd venture back out to the soda fountain for ice cream," Roxanne says as if having a craving.

Peaches barks, adding her comments to the conversation.

"Peaches," I whisper shout, ordering her to obey.

Lexi says, "What is a soda fountain, anyway? Is it the same as a soda jerk? Because there is neither a water fountain nor a jerk here. Well, there might be one of those next door."

I can imagine her looking up at me through those thick lashes as if challenging me. Yeah, I deserved that.

In addition to my general avoidance tactics, I'm guilty of a neighborly faux pas. Earlier this morning, I was coming back from walking Peaches. She was off leash since we were close to home. Lexi approached from the Penny Gamble and waved at us. The dog bounded toward her. I did my little trick to get Peaches to come right inside by saying the single word, *Treat*.

Torn between happy pets from a willing human and her favorite beef cookie, Peaches looked from Lexi to me and back again. I repeated, *Treat* and she reluctantly obeyed.

Lexi stood there, looking confused if not a little crushed. I told myself I'll let her think that I'm not a morning person rather than a jerk. Nan would've wanted me to be friendly, if not civil. But I'm not much more than a jerk.

"Sounds like you have a juicy story," Molly says.

"Tell us more," Roxanne adds.

I mentally beg Lexi to keep her lips zipped and not to feed the Pest Digest any gossip.

Then I summon Peaches by saying, "Treat," even it'll be her third today.

My triumph lacks luster as Peaches listens and bounds my way. I close the side door and order the part for the Duster before I can find out what Lexi said.

Chapter 8

Alive and Kicking

I t's mid-afternoon and something sweet wafts from next door.

Peaches returned to her post at the fence as if hoping for some crumbs. Either that or she thinks Nan returned.

I learned that Nan adopted the one-eyed dog during a lucid moment, early in her decline. Turns out that the corgi looked after Nan more than Nan looked after the dog. But they were best buddies.

I pat her head. "I miss her too, girl."

Tossing the ball across the sideyard, Peaches chases it. This section between Cory's shop and the soda fountain is the only area that I haven't gotten around to landscaping yet. I'm thinking of expanding my garden but am undecided if I want more strawberries or a place for a basketball hoop.

Because I also own half of the Penny Gamble, I've floated the idea of removing the fence and rebuilding it closer to the side of Cory's, so there would still be an accessway to my yard from the front. That would allow me to create a large patio area adjacent to the Penny Gamble for outside dining, music, and entertainment. You know, if I ever have time away from running the service station.

It isn't yet clear whether Lexi is staying or going. Then again, I'm still not done with her car.

I could blame the part for taking a while to get here, but I also couldn't stand to see that vehicle leave my shop in such shambles. Granted, Lexi kept the interior and exterior relatively clean minus a bit of road dust and crumbs. However, under the hood was a nightmare. The hoses were nearly blown, the brake pads were a molecule thin, and, suffice it to say, "Dusty," as Lexi calls it, needed some TLC.

Just then, Lexi says loud enough for me to hear, "This stockade fence is in desperate need of paint."

I go still and listen for sounds of motion to determine her location. It doesn't seem like she's on her side of the property. Rather, she's by the front entrance, meaning she's nearing my territory.

"Like everything else in this town, it's as if everyone has abandoned their positions and projects, neglecting upkeep and maintenance." She lets out a sigh as if the responsibility now weighs on her shoulders.

I'd like to say, *Yeah, like you did with the Duster?* But I hold my tongue because I'm not in the mood for a close encounter with the girl next door.

The bell on the office door to the shop jingles and Lexi calls, "Hello!"

And that's my cue to go grab some lunch.

I start toward the back exit. Peaches trails me as if disappointed playtime is over. As I sneak out the back, she looks at me with her puppy dog eyes and I toss her a treat.

She sniffs it and then turns up her nose before looking over her shoulder in Lexi's direction.

"Not going to happen, girl," I whisper before I make my escape.

I head a few doors down to the Laughing Gator Grille, sit at an empty table along the bank of windows, and order a turkey sandwich. I usually eat lunch at home but want to avoid Lexi—Cory would say the lengths I'm going to are extreme. I'd argue that it's mission-critical.

Gazing out the window, Lexi has a point. Nothing in Hogwash Holler has improved or changed since I arrived in town. It still looks like a battalion of swamp zombies beat up the buildings and structures.

Honey slides a plate in front of me. "Looks like you're daydreaming." She winks and approaches the entrance as someone comes in.

I'm not yet two bites into my sandwich when Lexi's smoky voice filters from the front of the restaurant. "His truck is in the lot, but he's not answering the door. Have you seen him?"

I'm facing them and would slouch down in the booth if that wouldn't make me look conspicuous.

Today, Lexi wears loose-fitting striped linen shorts that show off her legs and a muted red tank top. Her hair is down with little curls on the ends. I'm not sure whether she did it special or if the summer humidity gives them a bounce.

What is wrong with me? Why am I thinking about her hair again?

She says, "I'm locked out, and I think he has a spare key."

"Miss, I'm awfully sorry, but Cory is in the cemetery," Honey says as sweetly as she can despite the sadness that still permeates us all.

"You mean he's dead?" Panic streaks Lexi's voice.

"I regret to say it's true, miss."

"That's so tragic. I just saw him yesterday." Lexi blinks a few times.

Carl Soto enters the restaurant and stumps in my direction. In his booming voice, he says, "Hey, JQ, did you figure out why my scooter wouldn't start?"

Clearing my throat and trying to keep my voice down, I say, "Worn-out spark plug."

Carl is wide enough to fill a barn door but doesn't block me before Lexi spots me, er, hears me.

Her eyes go wide and she grips Honey's arm. With her other hand, she waves a frying pan at me. "Wait. You said Cory is dead. He's right there."

"Darling, that's JQ Ward."

"No, that's Cory from Cory's Automotive Service Station next to The Penny Gamble Soda Fountain."

Honey wears the same grief-stricken smile she always does when he comes up in conversation. "I grew up with Cory and I am quite sure that's not him."

"But—" Lexi sputters.

Meanwhile, everyone watches this interaction, which means it's sure to find its way onto the front page of the Pest Digest.

Lexi struts my way, still waving the cast iron pan.

Carl backs up, well aware this might turn ugly. But how could it? Lexi is so pretty.

My insides tick and twitch at the thought, and if I were standing, I'd take a knee because I need a break, a time-out. I'm afraid this is going to get out of hand. That my thoughts already hit that bump then kept on speeding despite precautionary measures.

"So you're not Cory?" Fire lights in Lexi's eyes as she juts the pan at me like she's brandishing a knife.

I give my head a slow shake.

"You're JQ?" Her mouth opens and closes as if preparing for a verbal assault.

I nod, shoring up my defenses.

Hip cocked, she says, "Why'd you let me think you're Cory?"

With a casual shrug, I cling to the hope that maybe if I don't engage, I can stall this firefight, I say, "It didn't come up."

"I've been calling you *Cory*." The pan in her hand wavers as if she's considering clocking me with it.

I frown. "Not to me you haven't." Though I am well aware, having overheard various conversations, that she thought that's my name.

"So, you're not Nan's grandson? The one she wanted me to marry?"

I nearly choke on an ice cube from the sip of sweet tea I took to cool things off.

Ah, that explains why she's been flirty with those long eyelashes and the cute little look she flashes when she waves at me...and speaks, except for right now.

Like we're going to solve this *mano-y-mano*, instead of having a heart-to-heart like on the ride into town, she shoves herself into the other side of the booth.

I wince when she drops the cast iron pan onto the table. It contains some kind of cookie cake with frosting or marshmallow filling. Not going to lie, it looks good, but there's nothing sweet about Lexi's expression.

"I was Cory's best—" It's still hard to say the words, even after all this time, but she cuts across me.

"Don't even try to worm your way out of this one."

"He left JQ the shop," Honey says as if strangely thankful it's not shuttered like so many other businesses in town.

Lexi narrows her eyes. "That would have been useful information to have, JQ, if that's who you really are."

Taking a bite of my sandwich, I say, "I didn't think it mattered."

"No, well, I—" As if not able to come up with a retort, she flounders.

"Can I get you something, sweetie?" Honey points at the baked good in the pan, "Or do you want some forks for that?"

"It was a peace offering to my neighbor who I thought was Cory Peterson. On second thought, I think I'll keep it to myself." She hugs the pan to her chest.

Honey pulls the serrated knife that came with my sandwich. Eyeing Lexi then me, she says, "Precautionary measure. She looks stabby."

"I should've read the fine print." Lexi huffs. "If I had money to pay for a lawyer, you'd be hearing from him, her, a whole team of attorneys."

"You'd sue me because I didn't tell you that I'm not—?"

"For impersonation. That's illegal. I've recently had to look into state and federal statutes and legal recourse, but that's beside the point. You—"

Having helped herself to a bite of the baked good on the table, Honey interrupts, "Yum, double yum. You made this?"

Lexi nods. "So one more time. Cory passed away, but JQ is still alive?"

"For now," Honey mutters with a mouthful.

"Still kicking," I say.

"You got that right. I feel like I was kicked in the gut. Why wouldn't you just say that you're not your dead best friend?"

Ouch. Lexi Dunn did not need a knife or a weapon to land a wound. She got me. Got me good.

The truth hurts and at the heart of it is that I don't have one. I'm broken. Not cut out for anything that approximates friendship, a relationship, or romance. I'm a selfish jerk and she should know that if she doesn't already. I take it she does.

"And JQ is one of the few eligible bachelors in Hogwash," Honey chimes in as if Lexi would even want my number.

I cast Honey a glare.

"You should give Lexi a tour of the town."

"How'd you know my name?" she asks Honey.

Honey chuckles as if that should be obvious. "Everyone reads the Pest Digest and has been observing your comings and goings. The sidewalk rendezvous, when you lean against the side of Dusty and watch JQ work. When he pokes his head out of the shop door to see if you're in front of the Penny Gamble washing those windows again."

"They're really grimy."

"It's like you two can't keep your eyes off each other."

"I didn't—" I start to say, but I cannot lie, only avoid the truth.

"Hogwash is a small town without much going on. At least, not anymore. Trust me, everyone and their grandmother is paying careful attention to you two," Honey says matter of fact.

"I wasn't—" Lexi starts, but then goes quiet.

Honey winks. "This is a hate-to-love-you kind of situation you got going on here."

"No, it's a neighbor war," Lexi says, declaring it right on the spot.

"Yeah, and it's on," I add.

"What about this little confection on the table here? I don't believe people who hate each other would bake for each other."

"I didn't bake anything," I say.

"I made it for myself," Lexi says as if that makes any sense, considering she came here with the pan.

"JQ, we both know that it doesn't take a week to fix a failed water pump for the coolant system," Honey says, instigating this wildly out-of-control conversation.

"The radiator fan was also busted," I mutter.

"Are you really a mechanic?" Suspicion laces Lexi's smoky voice.

Honey laughs. "He really is. Fixed my Porsche after I got a little carried away off the track." Honey takes another bite of the cookie cake thing. "What's this called, anyway?"

"It's an Original Lexi Dunn Sm'ookie."

"A Sm'ookie? I like that." Honey smiles. "You're neighbors and the neighborly thing to do is to give Lexi a tour of Hogwash."

Hands across my chest and sandwich forgotten, I say, "I'm not the town welcoming committee."

"True, we don't have one of those anymore." Honey scoops up a third bite of the Sm'ookie. "Oh, this is heavenly. Wow. Wow. Wow. You have to try it, JQ."

"Aren't you supposed to be working?" I say, hoping to get rid of Honey.

She arches an eyebrow. "Aren't you supposed to be getting good and done with the past?"

"That was bold," I mutter.

"He meant a lot to me too, you know," Honey says softly, referring to Cory.

Lexi looks between us as if not quite following. I'm in no mood to explain.

Honey says, "JQ, I'll give you a fork to try the Sm'ookie if you get out of your own way."

"I don't want to play nice." My voice is practically a growl.

Lexi crosses her arms in front of her chest. "Me neither. I want to play jerky."

"There isn't going to be any playing anywhere until you both kiss and make up."

"What?" we both ask at the same time.

Honey flashes a devious smile. "You'll be kissing before the week's out. I guar-an-tee," she sing songs.

This means there's a bet among the locals with my name on it. Last time this happened, they wagered that I wouldn't last a week. If nothing else, I can endure, so long as I'm left alone.

"No, we won't," Lexi says as if she'd rather kiss a frog.

"Definitely not," I agree because I don't want those pretty pink lips on mine. No way.

"Put your money where your mouth is and try this Sm'ookie. If you think it's gross, you're off the hook. No town tour. If it's delicious, show the gal around, then come back in a week and give me an update. Mama needs the performance exhaust kit upgrade for my Carerra."

"This is not how bets work, Honey," I say.

"I'm not typically the type to wager," she counters.

Lexi's attention swings between us as if she's missing a vital piece of backstory.

Honey was Cory's high school girlfriend.

I exhale and pick up the fork. "To be clear, I'm doing this for Cory."

Honey sniffs at my stubbornness.

I take a relatively small bite of the Sm'ookie just to indulge the two women. But that's more than enough.

This. Could. Change. Things.

The Sm'ookie is everything you want from the classic campfire S'mores treat but combined into a cookie with a crunchy, flakey, base beneath a non-gooey marshmallow middle that's still soft, and topped with a light chocolate chip cookie. It has layers, much like Lexi. Much like this situation.

I've left Hogwash and am in heaven.

With her dark blue eyes, Lexi watches me carefully.

"Yep, he likes it," Honey says as if there were ever any doubt.

"I see the smize." Lexi slaps the table triumphantly.

"Say what?" I take a sip of water.

"You don't smile with your mouth. You smile with your

eyes." She peers up at me through her long lashes, pleased with herself.

Honey inhales sharply, "You're right. I think you and I are going to be great friends, Lexi Dunn."

I can't help myself, drawing the pan closer, I take another bite of the cookie, er, Sm'ookie.

"He likes it," Lexi says.

Fine. Honey is right. I like it—and maybe the person who made it as well, but not too much.

Chapter 9

When Pigs Fly

LEXI

I repeatedly glance at JQ as we stamp—stomp?—along the sidewalk through town.

He's not Cory, Nan's grandson. He's Cory's best friend, but I don't think his reason for not telling me was as simple as it being irrelevant.

"That's the dumbest thing I've ever heard," I mutter to myself.

"What was that?"

"Oh, well, uh—" I'm about to fib to cover my tracks, but that would make me no different from him. Instead, I say, "I noticed when you and I were in the soda fountain the day after I arrived, you looked, well, I couldn't put my finger on it. There was some kind of emotion there."

"I don't know what you're talking about." His tone is airy, vague. Maybe he truly doesn't or his emotions are buried so deep, he'd need a trench shovel to unearth them.

"I thought that maybe being in the Penny Gamble was a painful reminder that you'd lost your grandmother when it turns out you also lost your best friend."

He grunts and then gestures to the This & That, a store that I learned sells a little bit of this and a little bit of that.

Using my very best radio voice, I say, "Need a ponytail holder? They have it. A toilet bowl cleaner? That too. A potato ricer? You got it." And if you're looking for a sink faucet replacement because you broke it off, they have you covered. I leave that part out. I've been tuning into plenty of Designed to Last episodes because the This & That doesn't quite quench my retail therapy needs and someone had to fix the efficiency's bathroom sink..

"I thought you were upset that Nan left her special place to a veritable stranger when she left it to two strangers."

Stabbing the air, JQ points, "Library, town offices, and the police station."

"Most town tour guides include fun facts, but that isn't the conversation I'm trying to have with you."

He abruptly stops. "So, you read the will and other documents?"

"I did indeed. Now I know it was Nan's wish that we fix up the Penny Gamble together."

"Is that what you want to do?" he asks with an air of disbelief. Before I answer he starts walking again.

Catching up to JQ's long strides, I say, "I haven't decided yet. It's not like I'm eager to volunteer to work with someone who hates me."

"I never said that. Honey did." Once more JQ pauses on the sidewalk and pushes up his sleeves, revealing blue-black tattoos that nearly reach his wrists.

"You never didn't say it."

"You declared war. If you're not aware, I'm a retired Navy SEAL, professionally trained for battle, Lexi."

"I didn't know that because you were impersonating a dead person, Mr. Tough Stuff." Having paused on the sidewalk like we're going to face off right here, right now, I stab him in the chest. Oof. My finger smarts.

Giving his head a dismissive shake and moving on, JQ says, "That used to be the Hogwash Hairwash & Style before they moved down the street. Now it houses a gaze of raccoons."

"A what? I don't particularly want to look at raccoons."

"A gaze, like a gaggle of geese. A flock of sheep."

Remembering that he's giving me a tour, I say, "Noted. Anyway, you infuriate me." In a confusing and dangerous way. He kind of makes me want to stay in town—not because I'm a glutton for grumpy guys. It's closer to curiosity. Perhaps accepting an unspoken challenge. Or it could just be I don't have anywhere else to go. But I keep that to myself too.

Letting out a resigned breath, JQ says, "It came to my attention that Nan was in cognitive decline, hence the state of the Penny Gamble."

"I had no idea." A double twinge of sadness pierces my heart. For Nan and for JQ—seems they were close.

"She needed care. Cory was her last living relative. He and I were like brothers. It was my duty to come here and help." JQ's dark brown eyes soften and the sunshine lightens his hair a shade, making him look slightly less big and bad, and more like a kind of guy who cares about people.

Maybe he does have an emotional range.

"So, you retired? For Nan?"

He shrugs.

"Is the apartment so tidy because you're a military man?"

"I can also sew and tie seventeen different kinds of knots underwater."

He has me in knots, that's for sure.

JQ continues walking with long strides and what I notice is the slightest, ittiest, bittiest limp. Over his shoulder, he says, "What else did you hear about me?"

Wait a second, we weren't talking about what I'd heard about him. Does that mean he's angling for me not to storm off in a huff? Maybe it's a tactic to win this war. Then again, I declared it. That means I'll finish it. Hurrying to catch up, I say, "That you like marshmallows."

"Who told you that?"

"You did."

He frowns, which isn't much different from his regular, all-purpose expression. "I did not."

JQ points out a theater with a broken marquee that I'm pretty sure is meant to read *When Pigs Fly Theater*.

"You liked the Sm'ookie, so you like marshmallows, which technically was a thank you for towing my car."

"You're welcome." JQ's tone is flat.

"You have a nice mouth—when you're not swearing from the garage," I quickly correct myself and cover my tracks with a nip of sarcasm.

The truth is his mouth is super nice with a lower lip slightly bigger than the upper—just about the only soft-looking thing about him. Well, the eyes too. Those aren't too bad.

He snorts. "And there I thought we were getting along."

"Not a chance, JQ. You lied." No way am I backing down either, Mr. SEAL Man Soda Jerk.

"I omitted."

"You lied," I repeat.

"I neglected to clarify a point."

"You lied," I say, unrelenting.

"I didn't correct your assumption."

"You lied."

"Listen, I'm not a liar."

"I never said you were. If you were listening, I said you lied. I try to be very precise in the words I choose."

He rakes his hand through his hair. "You're a complicated woman."

"Not really. Just hoping that you'll take responsibility for what you did." I stop because right here on the sidewalk is as good a place as any to get this over with.

"You want to me apologize?"

"Don't sound so incredulous. That's not an unusual request after lying. It would be a start unless you're genuinely not sorry. Honesty trumps a fake apology and if that's the case, the neighborhood better buckle up because the neighbor war is on."

"What will that entail?" JQ crosses his arms and leans casually against a cement wall as if he eats war for breakfast.

"Wouldn't you like to know? I'm not going to the war room with the enemy and tell you my secrets."

He makes a snorty grunt and then continues walking. I follow for no other reason than I'm not letting him out of my sight—the whole keep your enemies close thing.

We've reached the end of Main Street and are slowly walking down a long driveway bordered by Live Oaks and dripping with Spanish moss. It's lovely, but also lonely.

"Where are we going? Don't tell me you're going to dump me in the swamp."

"Do you mean the public swimming pool? That would be back that way at the community center." JQ gestures over his shoulder.

"Residents of Hogwash consider the swamp a suitable community pool?"

"No, but things changed here."

Before he can tell me what, I ask, "What's that?"

A large crystal mug leans against a shed. It's almost as tall as me. Emblazoned across one side with once-sparkly rhinestones are the words, *Root Beer.*

"That was the world's largest rotating root beer mug," JQ

says as if it's not the oddest thing to see when trespassing down someone's driveway.

"Interesting location choice, considering it appears as if we're venturing into crocogator territory."

"It used to be on top of The Penny Gamble Soda Fountain."

"Did it break?"

"It was stolen and then recovered."

"Which is why it's here, in the woods? That doesn't make sense. If it was stolen then recovered, you'd think the owner would put it away for safekeeping."

"Some people say the Boot Beer Boys originally took it. Others said it was lost in a duel. No one knows really except that Nan didn't put it back up after she took over at the Penny Gamble."

I stop. "What or who were the Boot Beer Boys?"

"Prohibition-era brew runners."

"Sounds like the Wild West."

"The wild south."

In the distance, a once grand antebellum home appears from the misty air. It hosts six columns supporting two stories with wide porches on the top and bottom. Moss and ivy creep along like fingers looking for something to tickle or take. There's a widow's walk at the top with a broken weather vane on the cupola.

It's a combination of Greek revival architecture and a fortress. I admire what were once ornate details and carvings along with the fortifications of someone expecting an invasion. It's nothing short of spectacularly spooky.

I stop and grip JQ's upper arm. My fingers don't quite wrap around the toned muscle. He looks down at my hand. I should pull it away. I don't.

"If you're wondering, that's Tickle Chateau."

"Tickle Chateau? Sounds humorously haunted."

"It is."

I step closer to JQ. "I thought you said there's no such thing as ghosts."

"I said the soda fountain isn't haunted. Remember, precision with words."

"Touché."

"No one really knows what became of Old Man Tickle except that one day rumors spread that he'd passed away. Then his grave appeared in the town cemetery."

"Ooh. A spooky story. But if that's the case, I'm going to get the swamp ghosts on my side."

"In our neighbor war?"

"Yep. Careful if you fall asleep." I wiggle my fingers down his arm and our hands brush. His are rough and hard.

I swallow at the feeling of popcorn kernels bursting inside me. Must be my trigger finger itching to go into battle.

Yet dappled sunlight filters between the leaves and paints the long dirt driveway in wavering patches of gold. Under this canopy and standing beside JQ, my shoulders relax for the first time since leaving Nashville. Forget knots, I'm like two fists punching each other. It's all terribly at odds with the hate I tell myself I feel for him.

Maybe I am a complicated woman.

JQ's low, rumbling voice reaches me as if through time. "Hogwash was once home to numerous roadside attractions."

"Like the Parthenon in Tennessee?"

"Never been, but that sounds about right. Here, they had the world's smallest chicken coop. Not to be outdone, there is also the world's largest coop. However, I think both structures are little more than kindling now. You'll also find a nest made entirely of peacock feathers collected from within our town limits. Supposedly, Tickle an affinity for the birds and then the things went and reproduced. There were many more, including the giant rotating mug of root beer—ours by the way."

"Why though?"

"Residents wanted to take advantage of the tourists and treasure hunters passing through."

"Tourists and treasure hunters?" I emphasize the last two words.

"Long ago, Hogwash Holler Township in Cameron Parish was known for farming, fishing, and thieving, but the main attraction was the hunt."

"Parish?"

"In Louisiana, it's roughly the same as a county."

I nod, vaguely recalling that regional geography fact from grade school. "Is thieving another word for hunting? Like deer, turkeys, and elk or whatever it is y'all hunt down here?"

"No, a hunt as in a scavenger hunt."

Recalling being stranded on the side of the road, I shiver. "Like vultures?"

"No, like treasure. Corsairs and buccaneers."

"Pirate treasure?"

"The Metairie Stronghold, an old fort, is still back there behind Tickle's property. It protected farmers from pirates sailing around these barrier islands."

A startling, squabbling sound comes from our left.

"What was that?"

"Wild turkeys, chickens, peacocks, probably. Maybe it's the albino crocogator warning us not to trespass on its property."

"Or ghosts?"

JQ lifts and lowers a shoulder like he can't be bothered by things like fear. "Could be swamp zombies."

"That's not helping." I shift yet closer to JQ and his warmth is like a warm nap or it could be the thick air hanging around us.

If anything comes at me, I'm using him as a shield. Also, I don't entirely mind the warmth that spreads through me when I'm this close. It's as addictive as candy.

"I'm talking about treasure like the Dubois Diamond and the Roger Cahoot Ruby—those were gems that Tickle's buddies had. When he and the two other Boot Beer Boys went their separate ways, supposedly, they each took a treasure."

"So, there was a third one in Mr. Tickle's possession?"

"No one knows what it was or what it was called, but supposedly he left five tokens hidden in town—Tickle's Golden Tokens—that would somehow lead to the treasure."

Piecing this together, I say, "That's what people hunt for and none of them have been found?"

"It's a load of hogwash if you ask me."

We're a stone's throw from the house. Vines climb the side as if the bayou seeks to reclaim the wood. Maybe even Tickle's hidden tokens and his portion of the treasure, if it's real.

A whisper of curiosity shivers through me. "Tickle's Golden Tokens?"

"Got the frissons, eh?"

It's cooler under the trees, but JQ must be sweltering in his duck pants and button-down shirt mechanic's uniform. "The friss-whats?"

"Goosebumps."

Rubbing my arms, I say, "I guess so. Where'd you learn about all this?"

"Cory. We'd be on patrols, night watches, and days of travel. Lots of long hours. He'd entertain me with tales from back home. But he also said that you can't believe everything you hear in Hogwash," JQ says.

"If that's the case what you said about ghosts went in one ear and out the other."

But I have to admit, I'm curious now. I'd like to see Hogan Tickle's grave.

Leaving the Tickle Chateau behind, we're both quiet as we make our way back through town. It's if we're each contemplating what's next in our battle strategy. Swords and daggers? Trebuchets and catapults?

Either that or JQ used up his allotment of words for the day. After all, the guy is the strong, silent type. Also, tall, dark, and handsome, but that's not a winning way to think.

Standing between Cory's place and the soda fountain, we're about to part ways, but we both hesitate.

"Update, the pump for the Duster won't be in for a few more days and I'm sorry." He points toward the sign with his best friend's name. "Truly."

I nod. "Thanks for both, but that just means you're stuck with me for a little longer."

With a soft snort through his nose, JQ walks away.

I can't help but wonder if all that talk about ghosts were cold war tactics to give me the *frissons*...or if things between us are heating up.

I'm leaning toward the latter because although JQ doesn't smile with his lips, those eyes don't fool me. Not with that rare smile of his. Nor can I keep pretending that those lips aren't ones I'd hate to love to kiss.

Chapter 10

Coming Swoon

LEXI

I'm going on week two in Hogwash Holler and the air seems thicker each morning. Every day threatens stormy weather, but most of it comes from next door where JQ and his potty mouth work on cars.

I stand outside the Penny Gamble with a handful of nails and a hammer, trying to figure out the exact placement for this sign.

Honey approaches with a baby wearing a sunhat in her arms. "Hey, Lexi. You look lost."

"More like humid, soggy, and about to make one of the biggest decisions of my life."

"I'm not sure I can help you with that exactly. I unexpectedly have my hands full. However, if you come by the Laughing Gator Grille later, I'll save you a po' boy and we'll get it dressed however you like."

Without meaning to, I glance at Cory's Automotive Service Station next door.

"I don't mean that kind of boy, though I'd argue he's a man.

I was talking about grabbing a sandwich. Today we have crawfish, and by dressed, I mean with lettuce, tomato, pickle, maybe some remoulade sauce to spice things up." She waggles her eyebrows.

"So, what's the deal with JQ?" I ask, cutting to the point.

"I'd ask for your Sm'ookie recipe in exchange for an answer, but I only play dirty on the race track. Everyone in town wants to know what's going on with you two."

"Is it their business?"

"In the past week, you guys alternate between looking like you're going to burn down your respective businesses and gobble each other up on the sidewalk. I tell ya, I have whiplash between the hot and cold."

"He said you and Cory were high school sweethearts. Does that mean you knew JQ too?"

"Not any better than I do now. They met on their first day in the service. Cory wrote me letters every week. Emails every other day. Texts by the hour when he could. Those two were as thick as thieves, I tell ya." She bounces the baby. "Cory done stole my heart, yes he did."

I don't think that was for me to hear, so I stick to the conversation. "JQ mentioned something about the Hogwash Hunt."

She puffs her cheeks. "That's ancient history, same as Cory and me. I still miss him. We were going to get married. He was gone too soon."

"But you're happy now. You found someone else."

"If you mean this bundle of joy, I suppose so." She nuzzles the baby and makes happy noises of affection.

I haven't thought too much about having a family, but I could imagine raising one in a small town like this, if the residents would spend less time reading the Pest Digest and more time sanding and painting their stores and homes, which is what I aim to do.

"JQ said there are a bunch of riddles on Hogan Tickle's grave."

She rolls her eyes. "If you're curious, go see for yourself, but you'll be disappointed. On the other hand, what I can tell you about JQ is that he was a good friend. Blames himself for what happened to Cory but don't believe it for a second. I've tried to tell JQ that Cory had a rare heart condition. Somehow it slipped past the medical evaluations. No one except Nan and I knew. I begged him not to enlist, but he wanted to more than anything. I don't blame him. I'd have left Hogwash if I had the chance." Honey looks around as if seeing the forgotten backwash town for what it is. "I don't know what, other than hope, keeps me rooted here. Cory isn't coming back. Toward the end, Nan forgot that."

"I'm sorry. Though I'm glad we met and Cory seems like he would've been a nice friend too."

"I'm glad you're here. I trust that Nan, and even old Hogan Tickle, had a plan."

"I wasn't sure about this place at first, but I see potential. And it isn't like I have anything more important to do than fix this place up."

"You have handy skills?"

"None, but I have a bucketful of determination and a business partner if," I raise my voice because a moment ago I heard Rolling Texas Thunder calling for Peaches, "if he'd get his butt over here to help."

"Oh, that man is wound tighter and stubborner than the town clock. The thing is only right twice a day."

"You're telling me, though I prefer to hear him sweet talking than the spray of profanity when he drops a greasy wrench."

"My bets are on the two of you. I'm going to get this munchkin out of the sun and leave you to your lovers' quarrel."

"Ha ha. We're not in love. We're at war, Honey."

"The Pest Digest readers already voted on a wedding date."

My jaw drops at the same time JQ appears, wearing a T-shirt, a first. His arms are tan, toned, and tattooed. I close my mouth and swallow hard.

Honey waggles her eyebrows. "I will be going now. Don't want to see this sidewalk go up in flames with me on it." Baby in arms, she scuttles off.

My cheeks blaze.

JQ scowls. "As I said, don't believe everything you hear."

Fanning my face with the folded canvas banner in my hand, I say, "I don't know what you're talking about. I haven't been flirting. I don't date and marriage is off the table. Who said anything about 'til death do we part?"

"Not me."

"Exactly. However, if you want to help me get this posted, that would be great." My voice is an octave higher than usual.

I never got famous enough in Nashville to become part of the local chatter, whether in person or online, but the Hogwash Pest Digest makes me want to crawl under a rock or head north because this kind of scrutiny makes me feel like an ant under a magnifying glass.

JQ and I won't ever kiss, and we certainly won't be getting married. No way.

I unfold the banner I found at the bottom of a bin at the This & That.

"What do you have there?" JQ asks.

With a little, "Ta-da," I reveal it, but there's a misspelling, which explains why it was at the This & That.

"Coming Swoon?" He chuckles.

"Just please help me hang it up." I open the ladder and position it in front of the door.

"You're not authorized to do that."

I step up a rung so we're face to face. "By whose authority?"

"The fifty percent co-owner. Didn't you read the papers?"

"Yes, however, the co-owner hasn't risked his life trying to remove the giant spider webs from the ceiling or unclog the toilet. He hasn't scoured the thick coating of grime from every surface only to reveal a sub-layer of filth. Nor did he have to contend with a very stubborn cabinet that refused to close, possibly verifying this place is haunted."

"I've been busy."

"You're being salty."

"You didn't attend Nan's funeral."

"Are you serious? I didn't know she'd passed away."

"Yet you came here to collect."

My hand flies to my hip. "You've been here so long you're just wary of outsiders. If you haven't noticed, I've been making an effort, which is more than I can say for you."

"I fixed your car."

I stumble a little and reach for the ladder at the same time JQ reaches for me. Never mind flames, the sidewalk could be lava with the way his touch sends a surge of warmth through me.

Our eyes catch for long enough for a fuse to be lit. But what will it mean?

"My car is fixed?" I stutter.

"You're free to go."

I narrow my eyes. "When did you finish fixing it? You've been working on a mommy mobile minivan all day today. Yesterday you had a Dodge in there and the day before that it was Mr. Soto's scooter."

"As I said, I've been busy." JQ tilts his head. "Have you been watching the shop?"

"Like a hawk."

"Why?"

I lengthen my spine. "Reasons that are none of your business."

More like watching the mechanic. It's hard not to when I take a daily walk through town to the Tickle Chateau and try to figure out how to get the giant crystal root beer mug back here. Also, if a ghost happened to come along, I would solicit its help in spooking my neighbor, just a little bit as revenge for telling all those tall tales...and aggravating me so much.

"We're partners. Of course, it's my business," he says.

"JQ, I came here because..." I debate how much to tell him. "Because I didn't have anywhere else to go. I hit a low spot."

"Ha, so you admit that you just came for the money."

Clenching my teeth, I say, "I didn't even realize there was money until last week, so no. But I am going to get this place to shine again. Breathe new life into it."

"Good luck."

"No, not good luck. You're going to help me."

He whirls. "I'm what—?"

"You're going to help me."

"I'm the one that gives the orders."

"No, we're partners. You said so yourself. Whatever this is, you've been alone too long. It's what Nan would've wanted."

"You hardly knew her."

"It's what Cory would've wanted."

JQ's face falls. His nostrils flare. For half a second, I'm afraid he's going to charge like a bull, but then his expression flickers. "You're right." He closes his eyes, inhales, and then repeats, "You're right."

"See you at seven."

"Until tomorrow." He waves as if eager to get away from this increasingly sticky situation, and I'm not talking about the humidity.

"I mean tonight. You can grill me something and we'll game plan."

"Now, you're pushing it, Lexi."

And I will continue to do so until he goes right over the edge. After all, we are at war. But maybe we're not fighting against each other. Perhaps, we're fighting for each other.

Chapter 11

Dustin Bruber

The next week is a rollercoaster of wins and losses.

On the practical side, Lexi tries to DIY everything. Only half of her projects are successful. I sweep up her messes.

On the side that I'd rather avoid, we get along about half the time, otherwise, we're like water and oil. I blame myself for letting her coax me into this poorly advised partnership. But she routinely reminds me we're doing it for my best friend and his grandmother.

She isn't wrong. But I'm afraid of what it will mean if I acknowledge that she's right.

With some of the projects, we'd probably be better off calling professionals. I'm handy with a wrench and socket set, but not the first on the list to hammer and nail.

Yet, with some HLTV how-to videos, we manage to repair shelving, de-squeak all the doors, remove lime deposits from the sinks, fix the toilet flush arm, and unclog the commercial dishwasher—we shall never discuss the snarl I pulled out. It may have had a tail.

She also tells me she contacted one of the shows on the HLTV network called Designed to Last, pitching Hogwash Holler as a candidate for a townwide makeover. I'm not exactly sure how that works, but it's not incorrect to say this little corner of Louisiana has had a makeunder, what with the treasure seekers.

After years of people leaving the place worse than they found it, everyone just gave up on making improvements. Though Nan had her own reasons; grief and a deteriorating memory had much to do with the state of the Penny Gamble.

As another week passes, it's like Lexi and I take two steps forward and two back. Just as soon as we get the soda fountain to make bubbles, the thing fizzes and is on the fritz. When all the soda syrups arrive, we store them as instructed, but less than two days later, they've gone bad and taste bitter rather than sweet.

And that pattern holds with Lexi and me too, and yet, from what I've heard, the Pest Digest is taking bets about firsts—when they'll see us holding hands, kissing, and tying the knot.

Also, she seems to hate country music, well, that one particular song that came on the radio the first day in my Land Cruiser. "I'd Run into the Storm for You." It must be her breakup song. She doesn't mind if songs by my cousins' band, the C.o.w.b.o.y.s. play.

Whoever hurt her owes her a song.

One afternoon, I walk into the Penny Gamble to find Lexi holding a baby. I see Honey pretty much every day and she wasn't pregnant, so I'm not sure how she came to have the child and she won't talk about it. All the same, my chest does something weird while Lexi brushes the baby's nose with her finger and makes silly little sounds.

"You okay, JQ? Looks like you saw a ghost," Lexi says.

Not a swamp ghost. More like a ghost of the future. I press

my hand to my chest because it feels like my ribs crack open. This reminds me of what Honey said about Cory's condition. She claimed he probably wasn't taking his medication. He didn't want to be seen as weak or even believe that he required a lifetime supply of pills to keep his ticker going. But this sensation is deeper, it goes beyond the bones and muscles in my chest.

Honey's gaze slides from Lexi to me repeatedly. "I've never seen you with that look on your face, JQ. I think the thermostat is broken in here." Honey grabs the baby and hurries away.

"We just fixed it," I say plaintively.

Lexi's long lashes flutter, and I belatedly realize what Honey meant.

I don't think she's the one reporting to the Pest Digest. Honey isn't like that and it appears as if she has her hands full with a mystery of her own. She probably wants to steer clear of Molly and Roxanne to avoid speculation.

Instead of Lexi's sunflower scent, something putrid gusts my way. I sniff the air. "Do you smell that?"

Lexi discreetly wafts her shirt away from her chest. "Thought maybe the baby—"

"It's not you."

Moving around the room, she follows me like a bloodhound on the trail.

"Be right back." I hurry next door and return with Peaches who is all too happy to see Lexi.

The corgi practically mows her down with her stubby legs and she lowers to the floor. Her nubby little tail vibrates with pure glee.

"Who's the best girl in the world? Give me a *P*, give me an *E*, give me an *A*…" Peaches gives her big kisses with her slobbery tongue before Lexi can finish her cheer.

This woman is good with kids and dogs. Handy too. She

has a determined spirit, even if she ran away from whatever happened in Nashville. I'll admit that I like it. I like it a lot.

When the two are done with their little love fest, I call Peaches and send her to seek out the scent. Trailing the dog, I keep moving because I can't let myself linger on what grows between us. I don't trust myself to be left alone in a room with Lexi. So, I choose the least mature tactic: teasing and distance.

"Smart to get the dog," Lexi says.

"Your hat isn't." I flick the brim.

She smooths the loose hairs that poke out as she adjusts it. "What's that supposed to mean?"

"The Boston Bruisers? Everyone knows the Golden Suns are the superior football team."

She takes off the hat and looks at it as if seeing the team logo for the first time. "It isn't mine."

"Is it a This & That purchase? That sounds about right since they're lucky if they sell anything that isn't half broken." I'm not above trash-talking the rival football team.

"Actually, they're the best team in the, um, of all the teams."

It's right then that I realize Lexi is bluffing.

"Name a Bruisers player."

"Bruh-brui-ber. Dustin Bruber."

"That doesn't even make sense and Dustin Bruber isn't a person."

She sticks her tongue out at me. "You don't make sense."

"Admit you're not a Boston Bruisers fan."

She crosses her arms in front of her chest. "I'm their biggest fan."

"You're so stubborn."

"I prefer determined. And you're rather cocky."

"I prefer confident."

"You're even cocky about being cocky."

"Well, you're bossy."

"So are you." She huffs.

"Then we're not that different."

Peaches gallops into the room with something hanging out of her mouth. Looks shimmery like scales? That was the smell.

"Please don't say she ate an old fish." I sniff my dog. Yep. She did.

"What are you talking about? What is that?" Lexi asks, her eyes flicking from me to some fish skin and what appears to be an empty pack of gum in Peaches' mouth that she drops at my feet.

"Could be nothing or we may have a saboteur on our hands."

"You think so?"

I grumble. "A rotten fish in an air vent is the oldest trick in the book. I'm afraid Peaches may have eaten whatever was left of it."

"At least they left some gum to freshen her breath."

"Ha ha. It's empty, but she wouldn't eat that. Smells too good." I wave my hand in front of my face. "And her breath does not."

"But who would do such a thing? We'll have to keep watch."

I have an idea who but for now, keep it to myself.

"I don't want someone to ruin our hard work. Have you ever run recce?" I ask.

"You think someone is going to come in here with a wrecking ball?"

"Reconnaissance work."

Lexi shrugs. "I went to a Renaissance fair once."

I chuckle. With us, we can go back and forth with banter or we can set aside our egos and make each other laugh. It's not the worst situation.

Bumping her with my elbow, I say, "I recall you mentioning you watched my shop."

"I'll admit, I don't mind seeing the retired Navy SEAL next door flex his skills and his muscles."

I turn slowly toward Lexi, not sure I heard her correctly. "Did you just say something nice about me?"

"A compliment? I guess so." She gazes at the floor, bashful.

A warm feeling tickles inside because I can't think of a time when a woman said something about me that made me feel, well, anything other than irritated, insulted, or abashed. Most recently that was the same woman who just filled me with sunshine.

"You know, your resourcefulness, determination, and bombshell beauty are a welcome sight. I mean an asset to this operation."

"Are you trying to flatter me or trick me into confessing I'm the saboteur?"

"No, I mean, yes, I was flattering you, for real and it didn't even occur to me that you'd try to ruin your own business."

"Insurance money?"

"We haven't yet signed the binder. That's still on our to-do list."

The corner of Lexi's lip lifts and she bumps me back with her elbow. "I was teasing. Couldn't let us get too mushy, soldier."

But why not? Why am I fighting this attraction?

Chapter 12

Breaking, Entering &
Breakthroughs

L exi drums her fingers on her hip. "How exactly is our stakeout going to work?"

I let out a slow breath because I did not expect to think about getting mushy with Lexi. I clear my throat. "My buddy Shaw was an associate in military intelligence. Maybe he could help. He's also the original Boy Scout, though now he has a wife, Cora, and a few kids. He's mentioned coming down to visit."

"I think we need a more immediate solution."

She has a good point.

The sound of rain patters on the roof and the *Coming Swoon* banner whips in the wind. Peaches sits at our feet and shifts closer when thunder cracks. Can dogs chew gum? Probably not, but the corgi stinks.

"Could be the crocogator," Lexi says.

"That's a bunch of hogwash."

Lexi lets out a long sigh. "So is my thinking that I can run this shop."

"That's not true. Nan did it and her background wasn't in making sodas and sundaes."

Lexi perks up. "Actually, my friend Rose runs an ice cream shop called Queen's Cones in Liberty Lake, New Hampshire. I'll see if she has any tips."

"That's good thinking."

"For now, who would try to interfere with us reopening the Penny Gamble?" Lexi taps her chin. "Do you have any enemies?"

I snort. "Uh, yeah. More than a few, but thankfully they're overseas and probably couldn't find their way here."

"That sounds sketchy."

"How about you?"

"No one comes to mind." Lexi runs her hand along the counter as if contemplating and then she stops in the space where the granite ends and it opens to the area for customers.

Crouching down, she says, "I didn't notice this before."

With the storm driving in, the room is dim and I shine a flashlight on the floor.

She points to a penny sunken into the tile.

"It's glued in there. Interesting."

"Wish we could ask Nan if she knew anything about it," Lexi says.

"Yeah. My guess is it was the first cent Hogan Tickle made. You know how some businesses pin up their first dollar bill."

"Maybe, considering this is the *Penny* Gamble." Lexi stands up and continues her stroll as if surveying our progress. Peaches stays tight to her heels. "Nan's last wishes were for us to restore this place to its former glory."

"I think we're well on our way."

"Totally, but this wall over here is kind of boring. Do you know if there are any old pictures of Nan, Cory, or even Hogan Tickle around? Images from the old days so people could

84

appreciate where the Penny Gamble Soda Fountain started and where it is now?"

"I was going through the office the other day and came across some articles." As I guide us toward the back hallway, a *drip, drip, drip* interrupts the squeak of my boots.

"Oh no," Lexi says when I open the door to reveal water streaming from the ceiling and puddling on the floor. "But it's not even raining that hard."

"Must be a burst pipe." I spring to action to turn off the water main.

Lexi gets a mop and we do our best to clean things up, but the water keeps coming.

"Too bad we don't have the giant crystal root beer mug here. It would catch a lot of it. Kidding. But I do want to get it back on the roof," she says.

We manage to contain the water in empty garbage cans that we take turns emptying—a different kind of keeping watch than I'd originally planned.

With a glower toward Main Street, I say, "This has to be another instance of someone trying to ruin our reopening."

"Who? Why?"

"My guess is someone was up on the roof and came in through the crawl space."

"Could be a coincidence?"

Unlikely, but I don't want to scare Lexi. Puffing my cheeks, I gaze at the damp floor and spot another penny sunken into the cement in the hallway. "Check it out. Another one of those. I'm surprised we didn't notice them before."

"In our defense, it was a mess in here."

"Nan, couldn't keep up and before I got here, she'd have episodes where she'd search for Cory, leaving no stone or table unturned."

"That's sad. You must miss him too."

"Yeah." My tone turns tight. I guess you might say I've turned over a few stones in my grief, er, more like boulders. But what's worse is the river of guilt I carry that threatens to sweep me away.

"Honey mentioned he had a heart condition."

The guilt turns to anger and resistance. "Did she also tell you that it was my fault?"

Lexi shakes her head slowly.

Like a dam bursting, the words flow out of me. "We were on leave. Showing off for some girls, seeing who could jump from the highest point off the side of cliffs and into a lagoon below."

"But Honey said he had heart trouble. How was it your fault that it stopped?"

"I shouldn't have been egging him on."

"Maybe not, but did you know about his health? That the doctors said he must not have been taking his medicine."

"No, but I should've been a better friend. I should've known about it." Anger pours off me in waves. This is why I don't get close to people.

Expression creasing, Lexi says, "How if he didn't tell you? Listen, JQ, I get why you'd feel guilty, but blaming yourself doesn't honor his memory as your friend. He had flaws too. Maybe he should've told you. Perhaps that would've hurt his pride. Maybe if he could do it all over again, he'd have kept it to himself. But he made the choices he made. Unless you pushed him off the cliff—did you push him?" Her eyes widen.

"No, of course not. But we were both showing off and—"

"And you regret it. I get that. I have regrets too, but you can forgive yourself. It's okay. If he was anything like Nan, he'd want you to let yourself live again."

Her words come at me fast. I try to dodge them like bullets, but there's no avoiding the truth. Deep down, I know that hanging onto the story that it's my fault keeps Cory with me in a way.

She continues, "I say all this with love, JQ. Being here has given me some time to reflect on my life. Trust me, my ducks are not in a row—they're wandering all over the place. There are some stragglers. Some rush to the front. It's a real sight, so I'm not judging you either way."

I exhale a chuckle. "Thanks—" I'm about to say more but spot something shining by the door. "Look, another penny."

"We should go see if there are more."

I nod. "Good talk, by the way. I appreciate you, er, it."

She grips my shoulder. "Don't mention it, soldier."

That ticking feeling riffles through me, and for the first time, I consider what it might mean to move on.

We find twelve more pennies, but during the search, I'm looking less for shiny copper objects and more at Lexi. At her button nose, her chocolate cherry hair, and her full lips. We crouch together close, and I can't help but inhale her sunflower scent, reminding me of a fresh summer day.

I admire how determined she is, how self-aware, and at times, funny. At least, she knows how to humble a man. But I don't have the bandwidth to think about taking a chance. And I definitely don't deserve her, not even after the breakthrough about Cory.

Seated at an empty table in the otherwise empty soda fountain, we speculate on the meaning of the pennies, on the instances of sabotage and suspects, and life in general.

Before I realize it, three hours have passed. The leak slowed down and I grab us each a popsicle from the cooler—Honey brought them over. She said she's encouraging our hard work because she wants some competition for the Laughing Gator Grille.

"Could Honey be trying to ruin us?" Lexi asks.

"No, no way. Honey is the sweetest person and with a baby in her care, she'd never find the time to poke a hole in our ceiling."

"True facts." Lexi takes her popsicle and our hands brush, warm against the cold in my hand.

Strangely, it makes me shiver inside.

She unwraps her pop. "Oh, root beer. My favorite."

"I'd peg you for a fruity pop person."

"I'm a root beer girl."

"Fitting, since that's what made Hogan Tickle start this place."

The popsicles are the kind with two sticks, meant to be broken in half and when she does so, the way they split sends both pieces to the floor.

We make quick work of cleaning them up, and then I offer her half of mine.

"Thanks. We make an okay team, huh?" she says, tapping her half against mine like a champagne toast.

I'm afraid to let myself think about what could become of us working well as partners.

Lexi shivers, whether from the popsicle or from having thoughts like mine.

"Chilly?" I ask.

"I'm afraid to go to the cemetery by myself. I cannot help but wonder about the riddles on Hogan Tickle's grave. Honey is probably right and I'll be disappointed. You too, suggesting it's Hogwash, but it's hard not to see how the hunt brought so much to the town and then took it away, much like how fire can both provide warm and destroy."

I nudge my head toward the door. "Little known fact, I've never been over there. Let's go, partner."

It's later in the day than I'd like to be around graves, all above ground here in the bayou. Unlike a regular cemetery where you can see above the headstones, Lexi sticks close like she's spooked and afraid a ghost lurks around every corner.

Placed prominently in the back, which is also closest to the coastline with a just-barely view of the water in the distance, is a mausoleum with fancy flourishes. Under a peaked top is the name, *Hogan Darius Tickle.* Underneath is his birthday and the years: *1890-1963.*

It then says, *When Pigs Fly* followed by five unmistakable riddles. We take turns reading them at a hush.

"I would just as soon imbibe this root as take to the air and make a hoot. Look up and see me on the blocks the blocks made of pinkish rocks. You'll find me sketched there, most rectangular seldom square."

"Can't help but think it sounds like gibberish."

Next, *Take one from apple but none from tart. Find one in liver but not in heart. The last you'll discover in giant as well as ghost but never, ever in a roast.*

I tip my head from side to side. That one is kind of clever.

The third one reads, *I have a head and a tail. I can break, but I am not frail. If you feed me, I will plink, but don't you worry, I do not stink.*

If I weren't in a cemetery I'd probably laugh because it's goofy.

The second to last says, *You can hold me tight but not to cuddle. However, I prefer the muddle minus three especially if there's a puddle. I cannot sew or sow, but I am the latter and getting fatter.*

"Muddle minus three. What does that mean?" Lexi asks.

The last one reminds me of a childhood tale. *The story is that of the three, one lives in a house made of a tree. The other you could blow over, but not mine even though it's in a field of clover.*

Even I shiver because this is the strangest gravestone I've ever seen. What did Mr. Tickle intend? Is there really treasure?

Chapter 13

A Penny for my Thoughts

LEXI

The swamp ghosts aren't real. The zombies aren't real. The treasure isn't real.

Lying in bed, I repeat these words like a refrain, a tuneless song except to the beat of my pounding heart.

From the adjacent building, I've been hearing things. Each night, I try to ignore them. Could be ghosts, zombies, or treasure hunters.

They might not come in such great abundance, seeking Tickle's tokens, but who knows, perhaps teenagers dare each other to go looking late at night—my mother always said nothing ever good happens after midnight and it's five 'til.

When a series of rattles result in a bang, I toss off my sheet. Actually, I take it with me because if someone is sneaking around my store, I'm going to give them the scare of their life.

I'm not the kind of gal to turn into a pumpkin after midnight and I certainly don't have a glass slipper, but as the clocktower in town strikes the hour—the one time of day it's correct—I startle. But the sound allows me to open the back door to the Penny Gamble without alerting anyone. I pad down the long hallway, listening carefully.

If it's the saboteur, I'll scare them, wrap them in the sheet like a mummy, and then call the police. They'll never see me coming. With my ghost costume in place, the only thing I didn't consider was not being able to see. The cotton is relatively thin though, and I can discern shadows and shapes—the display case, the tables and shelves, the jukebox.

Floating forward and arms extended—mostly so I don't bump into anything, and so I can grab hold of whoever is in here, I listen carefully. The clock tower is now silent. So are the streets. From above, I detect a faint scratching sound, but with the sheet over my head, everything is muffled.

I continue forward then, getting into character, I let out a haunting "Hoo, hoo," sound. Quiet again, I listen.

Let's be real, I don't believe anyone would really think that I'm a ghost, but they'll be wary of a person who'd go so far as to dress like a ghost because like my mother also said, *Never get too close to someone who's missing a wheel from their apple cart.* I've never seen anyone with an apple cart, but I took the expression to mean to steer clear of crazy.

If there's a prowler in the Penny Gamble, they're going to think twice about crossing me!

When I remove the sheet, a pair of headlights cruise slowly past, illuminating the front window briefly. I blink a few times, temporarily blinded, but in that split second, I saw a flash, er, a glint of something.

Hogwash Holler doesn't see much traffic day or night and it's late. I wonder who drove by. Could be the roving pack of teenagers, could be treasure hunters, or someone returning from the late shift.

Or perhaps whoever was poking around here got spooked and made a relatively slow getaway. Then again, maybe it's my imagination. My mother's warning about nothing good happening after midnight did not exclude me from making bad and potentially dangerous decisions, like wandering around a construction site after hours. There are buckets of paint, piles of wood and tile, and other materials in here that pose a danger to a barefoot woman with a sheet over her head.

This might be what JQ meant about Hogan Tickle entertaining himself—it could be argued that this is the kind of situation I'd laugh at if I were inclined that way.

Well, not anymore which is why I see the bobbing of a flashlight coming close. Tingles rush along my spine. Ha! So I wasn't wrong. Someone is sneaking around.

I dash behind the counter to hide. Then I piece together the fact that I heard the noises from inside, checked, and didn't find anyone, and the light is coming from down the sidewalk in the direction of Cory's. Maybe someone else called the police and the prowlers fled. Or someone called the police on me!

I swallow a growing lump in my throat. "Next time, I'm listening to my mother about the whole midnight thing," I whisper.

Peering around the side of the counter, I take a peek. The silhouette of a large man with broad shoulders takes shape.

The tingles turn into twisty excitement and relief. It's JQ.

I admit, this wasn't my best move, coming down here with a sheet. He'll be the one laughing if he finds me here. Not going to happen. We have a ceasefire agreement in the neighbor war, but that wouldn't stop him from having a belly laugh at my expense.

On my hands and knees, I crawl toward the back door, avoiding the beam of light streaming through the window like a spy performing a graceful and elaborate acrobatic maneuver through a laser light field. At least, that's how I imagine myself.

The movement is probably more like a jellyfish moving through pudding.

Fully immersed in my role as a ninja spy, I accidentally leave the sheet behind. If anyone on the jobsite tomorrow asks about it, I'll tell them we'll use it as a drop cloth while painting. For now, I am not going back in there.

The only problem with that is when I get back in bed, nerves frazzled, I still can't sleep with my mind repeatedly flashing to the glint I saw through the window when the car passed by.

My thoughts float to the story about Tickle's Golden Tokens, which inevitably lands me on the handsome yet grumpy man who told me the tale.

I can't help but wonder if he was out on a hot date...and that notion makes me feel strangely and surprisingly jealous of the woman he held open the door for, shared a meal with, and potentially kissed goodnight.

Jealousy doesn't make for a good night's sleep.

The next morning, JQ arrives at the Penny Gamble jobsite with a ceramic mug in hand and wearing a plaid shirt. His manly scent of clove and spice caresses my nose.

"You smell amazing."

He tucks his chin.

My cheeks blaze. "I meant the coffee. Have any more of that golden bean juice?" It's unusually cool and I gather up the sheet, evidence that I was the late-night prowler. Now would be a good time to stuff it over my head to hide my pink cheeks.

"This was the last of it."

"You drank the whole pot?"

He surveys the space, eyes scanning our progress until they land back on me. One of his eyes narrows as if he senses something is out of place.

Belatedly, I add, "Or you don't want to share?"

"I used a French press, made enough for me."

"Aren't you fancy?"

He tilts his head in the other direction as if to say, *And aren't you so odd?*

A yawn escapes and I cover my mouth.

"By any chance, did you see anything unusual last night?" JQ asks.

My eyes shift from left to right, left to right. "Where?"

"Here?"

"Um, no. Nothing."

"I was out late and when I drove through town, I thought I saw—"

"Definitely not me. I was as snug as a bug in a rug." When I realize how dorky that sounds, I add, "My mom used to say that."

"You didn't hear or see anything?"

Unfortunately, no, nothing except him checking on the shop because his eyes didn't deceive him. Someone was in here and that was me, but I've crawled too far into this hole to reveal that I was down here, with the sheet in my hand over my head, because I was intending to scare a fellow ghost.

With a laugh, I try to play it off, but then my gaze catches on something shiny and round—the glint JQ's headlights caught when he drove through town, spotted me, and then came to investigate.

However, before I have a chance to take a peek, a loud bang comes from the back hallway and we both rush toward the door.

When we open the one separating the spaces, the outer one that's closest to my apartment slams.

JQ mutters, "I knew it," then races down the hallway.

He stops short on the threshold that leads outside. I run

headlong into his back, smooshing my face into his muscular frame and smashing my nose.

"Ow, ow, ow." Squishing my eyes closed, I hop as if that'll help alleviate the pain combined with the unique feeling like I snorted horseradish into my sinuses that comes when hitting my nose.

JQ turns to me and as if he didn't feel a thing, he asks, "What happened? Are you okay?" Then his eyes bulge. "You're bleeding."

Forgetting about the assailant, he rushes to the bathroom and returns with a wad of tissue. I catch a glimpse of myself in the mirror. Still clutching the white sheet, I look like the victim of a crime scene.

"I'm okay, promise. I bumped my nose on your unusually hard back. Do you have some major muscles back there? I'm prone to nose bleeds. Really, it's no big deal. Nothing to see here." I wave the bloody sheet. My rambling sounds nasal. The *M*s sound like *B*s and the *N*s sounds like *D*s. I look deranged like I walked off a horror movie set.

This is my cue to rush past JQ and into my apartment where instead of hiding under the sheet, I'll just crawl under the bed and never come out again.

And to be honest, after the late night and without any of his golden bean juice, I could really use a nap even though it isn't yet nine am.

Chapter 14

Singing & Snoring

A few days later, with the ceiling fixed and without any more clues about how it happened or who did it, my cousin Tucker calls. He lives down in Blue Bay Beach with his wife Chevy and their wild child crew. He's a car buff like me and has his own garage and numerous projects going at all times.

Tucker says, "We're meeting at your parents' house. You have to see Maybellene."

"Who?"

"A mint 1955 Coupe de Ville."

"You named the car?" That reminds me of Lexi and Dusty. Then again, she's never far from my mind.

"After a song Chevy likes. Anyway, the Ritchies are getting together and we don't want you to miss it."

"A family reunion?"

"A mini one. No way would we do one with the whole family unless it was at the ranch, but it's a good halfway point. Will you come out? Haven't seen you in a while."

"I've been—"

"What's that?" Tucker asks.

"You didn't let me finish."

"Because I heard a certain melody in your voice."

"A what? Tucker, have you been in the Florida sun too long?"

"No, I just recognize the sound of love and I've never before heard it in your grouchy old voice. So, tell me, have you been falling in love?" He laughs like there's something funny about love and then tells me about the Cadillac.

I suck in a breath and only vaguely hear him singing the praises of his fine restoration work.

"Your dad mentioned that you have an old Caddy at the shop. Maybe I can give you some pointers."

I have numerous old cars to restore, but those are long-term projects. More immediately, there's the soda fountain next door. I fill him in but don't say anything about Lexi even though she popped brightly to mind when he mentioned love.

"Wow, JQ the multi-business owner. You're moving up in the world."

"Technically, I'm a co-owner."

"You went in halfsies with someone? That's so not like you, a loner. Wait. Hold up. It's a she, huh? A woman. A lady. Tell me you met someone. JQ truly fell in love." Laughter fills his voice.

I stammer.

Tucker laughs. "I know what that means. Don't sweat it. We should all be so lucky to be bitten by the love bug. It can render us speechless, make blundering fools of ourselves, and help us grow and strengthen our resolve of what it means to be a man. Consider it an honor, cous.'"

I play the denial game before we make plans and get off the phone.

From beyond the fence, Lexi sings a familiar tune—one of

the C.o.w.b.o.y.s. songs. Her voice is alluring, all-consuming, and beautiful. I hardly hear whatever else Tucker says before we get off the phone. As she continues to sing, I stop in my tracks.

I've heard her voice before—and not just during this past month. I blink a few times, staggered. Lexi is the person singing on the CD that puts me to sleep every night.

I'd like to believe Tucker's comments about being struck by love's bugs or arrows or whatever and take it as a sign that it's meant to be, but doubt whirls inside, pushing me back, away from her and a potential future.

An alarm bell goes off like there's a raid and I freeze, which isn't something that's ever happened to me. I'm a trained combat soldier and know what to do in these situations, except right now. But this isn't war. At least not anymore. No, this is love and it's a battle I've never before fought. I'm afraid to lose. Terrified of what will change if we win.

After a beat of the alarm blaring, I realize it's an actual fire alarm, but I don't smell smoke. Likely, it accidentally went off.

From beyond the fence, Lexi mutters about the stupid alarm and a pesky fly as she calls my name. Thankfully, there's not an emergency. Phew. Crisis averted, but I still have my own on my hands.

Instead of rushing next door, I jump into my backyard hammock as she charges through the gate. I guess I want to seem casual as if I'm not freaking out inside. Tucker was right about me being a loner, except when it came to the SEAL Teams. We were solid. The thing is, I'm not used to emotions or anything having to do with the *L* word.

"JQ, I accidentally set off the fire alarm but can't reach it to turn it off. Don't worry, nothing is in flames and it wasn't the saboteur, although we got a piece of mail that looks suspicious."

Like a weirdo, I close my eyes and pretend to be asleep before she halts by the hammock.

"JQ, I'm sorry to wake you up, but I need someone taller or with a ladder. I loaned the other one to Roxanne a little while ago and keep forgetting to ask for it back."

I don't move. I'm frozen. Stunned still. I can't believe I didn't place her voice on the CD before now.

"Hey, sleepy head." She speaks softly as if she caught me napping.

My brother used to prank me by waking me up in the middle of the night, saying I was late for school. I am the master at pretending to be asleep. He'd try every trick in the book— feathers, ice water—nothing would get me to flinch.

"JQ? Seriously, I need your help." Her hair cascades over my face as she lowers her head to listen for my heart.

I force my nose not to tickle. I am a rock, playing possum, and I'm a wreck inside.

"You have a pulse," she says.

Thank goodness, but it's probably hammering with her so close, with her scent, and silky hair. *My* alarm bells are out of control.

"You have a lot of tattoos. I like them." She traces her finger along the anchor, the trident, and the names of my fallen brothers.

That pricks my ears and heats me up. I like her soft, sun-kissed skin. Her touch. Her voice. I like everything about Lexi Dunn.

She exhales. "How can you sleep through that beeping?"

Sure, I could fall asleep in less than thirty seconds when I needed shut-eye while off duty, but if the dog breathes wrong, I'm wide awake. Yes, she sleeps on the end of my bed. I can't resist that corgi.

"Maybe Peaches can help."

More like snuggle up. She's happiest when we're both stationary—or playing ball.

Nothing Lexi says gets me to relent. If I do, that means facing the fact that I care about this woman. A lot.

"Are you bald?" Lexi asks.

I nearly react. I most certainly am not. Although, I did find a gray hair a few weeks ago.

"Ew. I found a pustule on your arm."

Ah, I know what she's doing. My brother has tried this tactic too—say something outrageous or concerning to get me to break character. Not a chance. Then again, I'm not entirely sure why I'm doing this, other than the truth behind the conversation with Tucker.

"Stop snoring, JQ."

And there it is. The chink in my armor. I drop the charade and bolt upright, making the hammock rock precariously. "I wasn't snoring."

Lexi's topknot bobs on the top of her head as she plants her hand on her hip. "How would you know unless you were awake?"

"Because I don't snore."

"But it's impossible to know that unless you record yourself asleep."

"I don't snore," I insist.

"Then you were awake that whole time." Her lips ripple with a smile.

I can't rightfully explain what came over me. It's not like I was avoiding Lexi. More like avoiding myself when I'm around her. Who is this guy with feelings and desires?

But I'll make it up to her, literally. After shutting off the fire alarm and making sure nothing else is out of the ordinary, I go home and get to work.

First comes the homemade dough which needs to rise.

Next is the sauce and toppings. Oh, and let's not forget getting the pizza oven up to eight hundred degrees.

When everything is good and hot and cooking, she shouts over the fence, "Smells good."

"Come on over."

"You're inviting me to your place?"

I can't see her face, but I imagine adorable incredulity, complete with her hand to her chest in the classic *Who me?* gesture.

"Yes, you. Oh, and bring your bathing suit."

"I am not swimming in a swamp."

I chuckle. "Peaches wants you to join us for dinner." I thought saying that would make me feel better about this big step. But I want Lexi to know that I'd like her company too.

Chapter 15

An Oasis

L ess than sixty seconds after I holler over the fence, inviting Lexi into my oasis, the dog is barking an excited greeting and Lexi stands at the edge of my backyard, gobsmacked.

I say, "And I wanted to have dinner with you too."

Her smile is irrepressible, but she knows not to push it with the mushiness, otherwise, I might spook. "What you have back here is nothing short of an oasis."

"Exactly."

She takes in the pool, Jacuzzi hot tub, hammock, gardens, sauna, cold plunge, lounge area with the fire pit, and the grilling-dining space where the clay pizza oven is pumping out the fantastic scent of wood smoke, baking dough, and garlic.

"I call it home."

"A paradise."

"Make yourself comfortable." I offer her a drink and check the pizza.

I'm not sure if it's the setting or if Lexi and I have cleared an invisible hurdle, but our conversation comes easily tonight.

We discuss everything from the Penny Gamble Soda Fountain to strategizing how to get the crystal mug back on the roof to our favorite ice cream flavors to childhood pets and embarrassing stories from when we were teenagers.

I've never felt so comfortable talking with someone, not even Cory. And I want to know everything about her.

"So is Lexi short for Alexis or something else?"

"It's short for Lexington."

"That's beautiful." I wonder what would happen if I called her that?

"More like practical. My dad is from Lexington, Kentucky and my mom was born in Lexington, Massachusetts. It's like they didn't want to forget where they came from when they settled in Tennessee."

"What about you? Will you name your kid after your hometown?"

"I'm from Chattanooga, so no. But then we moved to eastern Tennessee. Mom and Dad live in the same house I grew up in."

"Mine too, but in Texas."

"Don't get me wrong, I love it there, but I went to New York just as soon as I could. I wasn't the best student. My English teacher said I was in a constant daydream. Not analytical enough. So, I was eager to make it in the arts. Started with painting then switched to singing. After less than a year there and I realized I was a little more down home than cosmopolitan. That brought me to Nashville."

"Same, well, not daydreaming, painting, or singing. But my head was already somewhere else by the end of freshman year."

Our gazes float together in understanding. Perhaps we have more in common than I thought.

"Turns out I could write songs pretty well though. Play

guitar too. I'm not sure where the talent or interest came from since neither of my parents are musical."

I get a flash of inspiration and say, "Be right back." I return seconds later with Cory's Martin acoustic.

Lexi's eyes widen when I tell her it was his and share a few stories about how he'd written songs for Honey. "He'd also write spoof songs for people's birthdays and special occasions. He was such a jokester."

"Sounds as if you guys were like brothers."

"Definitely. I also have a brother. John." I talk about my family and learn Lexi is an only child.

She grins. "There it is. You smile with your eyes when talking about your parents, John, and Cory."

"They're the good ones."

"You are too, you know." She inclines her head as if she dares me to disagree. Already, she knows me so well. Cory once teased that I'd rather take a bullet than a compliment.

With my elbow resting on my knees, I gaze at my hands. I want to refute her comment but take it in. Reaching for Lexi's hand, I braid our fingers together. She shivers at first as if unsure about what's happening, then softens as I squeeze her hand. Where I expect a flare of desire, a sense of peace washes through me. As I let out a long-held breath, I know with certainty that I want to shower this woman with compliments, praise, and love for a long, long time.

"Thank you, Lexi." My voice is low but confident as I enter unfamiliar territory.

"My pleasure. So, your parents live in Texas and you met Cory in the military, and now you're here."

"Cory and I would always talk about his beloved 1968 Dodge Charger, or as he called it, *The Super Charger*. He and Honey bonded over driving fast. Anyway, the shop was his father's, and he worked there growing up and planned to do the same when he retired from the military. His dad passed away when he was in high school. Bad liver. Nan took care of him. Well, she always did, but after that, they grew even closer. Some guys rebel after a tragedy. Not Cory. To my surprise, Cory left the shop to me."

"I take it you did rebel after the tragedy."

"Guilty. I stayed in the military though. Completed a lot of missions. Got wounded. Worked a desk job. Then learned Nan wasn't quite the same after she lost Cory. Like she was waiting for him to return. Eventually, she got forgetful. Neighbors would find her looking for him around town. Retired and came directly here."

"That was good of you."

"The least I could do. Nan and I would talk about Cory. Sometimes she'd think I was him. I don't know if this is right or wrong, but I didn't always correct her. It made her happy."

"Talking with you like this makes me happy." Lexi peeks at me from under her long eyelashes.

That warm frisson-like deep inside feeling that I've never before felt grows. "Lexi, I don't know if this is weird or not, but when I arrived in Hogwash, Nan gave me a CD. I listen to it before bed. Helps me sleep." I click it on now.

When the strains of the first song stream through the stereo, Lexi's face lights up. "That's me. Nan started sending me fan mail and things just went from there. I sent her that CD. You've been listening to me sing before bed?" Her voice is soft like she's flattered and not freaked out.

"I only made the connection when I heard you singing over the fence."

She gets still, listening carefully. "Wow. I haven't heard some of these songs in forever." She hums and strums the guitar as if remembering the lyrics and tune like riding a bicycle. It's amazing on the recording, but straight-up astounding live.

I take a risk and ask, "So, what really brought you here and away from funneling all this musical talent into shows and recording?"

"I wrote a song and then heard it on the radio."

"That's a good thing, right?"

"My ex stole it and gave it to my biggest rival—Suzie Lou LeMonde. I got no credit and can't begin to try to prove it. And now I can't write. Total creative block. I'll never come up with another song as good as that one."

"These all sound good to me."

She sighs. "Thanks, but—" She pauses, listening. "Hold up. Here it is. This is *I'd Run into the Storm for You.*"

I recognize it instantly and realize I've heard it numerous times on the radio. "Your version is different, more soulful. Better. And I'm not saying that because I'm biased."

She lets out a breath as if she too had been keeping it locked up in her lungs for longer than is advisable. "You know, I agree. Hearing it and knowing that it was originally mine makes the whole thing sting less."

"Glad I could help. So, it's not weird?"

"JQ, are you asking if you can keep the CD?"

I nod, feeling bashful.

She shifts closer, bringing her sunflower fresh summer day with her. "You may absolutely keep it, and I'll give you another batch of songs you might like."

Our eyes catch and sincerity shines between us.

"I'd love that. Could we listen to it at the Penny Gamble?"

Our hands join again and my pulse ratchets up a few notches.

"I think that would be okay. But I want to know, would this be okay?" She leans in and plants her lips on mine.

I inhale sharply. This woman takes my breath away. Everything except Lexi melts into the background as she leans into me.

I quickly conclude that her hair is far softer than I imagined. Her lips too and yet they're demanding, telling me she wants this kiss as much as me even though we both know it's probably not a good idea.

People say not to mix business with pleasure. But this feels so good. So right.

My breath remains suspended and we continue to kiss as if erasing all our disagreements, my cold distance, and her sassy stubbornness.

Everything we can't say to each other channels through now, with Lexi's hands on my back and mine carefully cupping her jaw and the nape of her neck.

At this moment, I realize how precious she is. A true treasure.

I pause and say, "Yes, this is definitely okay."

She lets out a soft little sound of contentment.

No, it's more than okay. It's everything I never let myself have and didn't know I wanted, all wrapped up in a pint-size ball of pep, sunshine, and deep blue eyes. One thing I know for sure. I'd run into the storm for Lexi.

Chapter 16

Hopefully in Love

LEXI

When my lips connect with JQ's, at first, it's like we're testing the waters, making sure it's not too hot and not too cold.

With him, it's just right.

After a strong and steady kiss, he goes rogue in the best of ways. His lips find the edge of my jaw, the little spot behind my ear, and then return the way they came. His mouth on mine is a caress yet demanding, unrelenting.

My pulse quickens. The world spins as if trying to catch up when the kiss deepens.

When his fingers graze my shoulders a liquid wave of longing flows through me. I fist his shirt, further closing the space between us. I go up in flames.

Kissing JQ is everything I hoped it would be and more. My heart on fire beats out a little rhythm of hope.

Remembering that until recently we were at war, I pause and say, "This is probably a terrible idea."

"The worst." He kisses me again.

Unable to resist, I kiss him back. "We shouldn't be doing this."

"Definitely not."

But we don't stop.

"Why aren't we stopping?" I ask.

"We really should," JQ says, trailing little kisses along my neck.

We don't as his mouth finds its way back to mine.

He pulls me closer and the kiss deepens, reaching all the way to my toes.

I hardly notice the sunset because it feels like something new is dawning inside me—feelings of hope, renewal, and a spark of something I haven't felt in a while. It's not just love, it's also creativity.

This kiss is so good, I could write a song about it. Maybe I should.

When we part, my heart races in circles as if saying, *Did you see that? Feel it? It wasn't just pleasant. It was phenomenal. Let's do it again!*

Okay, that last part was all me, but talking with JQ tonight, I appreciate our differences and also see that we're compatible in so many ways. Oh, and let's just say that he looks good in his usual blue shirt and heavy-duty pants, but JQ Ward is a treat in board shorts and a T-shirt.

A faint tune filters into my mind and I catch myself daydreaming about us, him and me, and what our melody would sound like.

Just then, he gets to his feet, tugs his shirt over his head, and tosses it on a nearby chair before diving into the water. The pool light ripples as he crests through the water. This backyard is but one secret that surprises me about JQ. The other is how easy he is to talk to now that we laid down our weapons and suspicions.

We make a good team. I like the idea of being business partners and then coming back here after a long day, sipping soda or sweet tea, and watching the sunset. That wouldn't be a bad life.

But could I stay in Hogwash? What about music? If that little surge of inspiration turns into an injection of creative motivation, I can't fathom making it in the country music industry anywhere outside Nashville.

JQ swims to the edge of the pool and wiggles my toes. "Coming in?"

I let out a sigh, leave thoughts of my future on the chair along with my sundress, and cannonball into the deep end.

We splash and play in the water like a couple of teenagers on their first date. It's fun and refreshing and something I'd like to do regularly, but as soon as I get out of the pool, the pending future sticks to me like the humidity in the air.

JQ gives me a fluffy blue and white striped towel. "Something on your mind?"

"Just life. The future. Big plans."

"Something that's always helped me is breaking all that down into little plans. Like bite-sized pieces." He sits down and the leg of his shorts lifts a little, exposing scarred skin above his knee.

"What happened?" I ask, unable to help myself.

"Eh, just life."

I slug him in the arm.

"Took a few bullets."

"A few?"

He swallows. "Five."

But the word comes with heavy punctuation like he doesn't want to talk about it right now. I relate because in much the same way he doesn't want to trudge through the past, I don't want to plod into the future and what my plans look like.

It's like we mutually agree to change the subject and discuss The Penny Gamble Soda Fountain, including what we want the menu to have on it.

We agree to take some of the oldies forward and toss around some new ideas like a cake batter milkshake, with sprinkles, of course, along with some holiday specials like egg nog. We also decide that the official name is The Penny Gamble Soda Fountain and Dessert Bar.

"And you definitely need to serve the Sm'ookie."

"You like my Sm'ookie?"

JQ leans in, brushing his nose against mine before nipping a kiss on my neck. "Lexi, I love your Sm'ookie."

I can't help but giggle.

After we kiss some more, JQ walks me next door. We linger outside, forefingers linked, swinging them between us.

"Tonight was really nice. Thank you for the pizza. By the way, if we can figure out a way to incorporate it into the menu, like Friday night pizza, I would not object."

"We'll see. That's a tall order."

"But it's a short walk from here to the pizza oven." I point between his place and mine, er, the soda fountain.

"There's a fence in the way."

"I think we could figure out how to take it down."

All evening, JQ has been smiling with his eyes, but I see one teasing his lips.

I kiss them one more time and then we say goodnight.

Just before I go inside, he calls, "I'm heading home to Texas for the weekend. Once we open the Penny Gamble, it might be a little while before I'll be able to visit again. Would you like to come with me?"

My answer is instant. "Yes, of course."

"We'll leave tomorrow afternoon to beat traffic." After a

pause, JQ says, "Sweet dreams." Then he disappears into the inky night.

Am I walking on clouds? Yes.

Am I replaying every moment of our kisses? Indeed I am.

Am I freaking out inside because I'm going to meet JQ's parents and not a single guy I've ever dated has ever asked me to go see his folks? Yep.

Chapter 17

Dating Not Hating

LEXI

The next morning, I wake up with one word in my head. *Dated.* I don't need a calendar to find out what day it is nor do I sense there is somewhere important that I need to be and forgot to write it down.

Dated is lodged in my brain because my last thought before I drifted off into JQ-filled dreams was about how not a single guy I've ever dated has ever invited me to meet his parents.

This begs the question. Are we dating?

Last night was unexpected in the best possible way. We shared a meal, which was delicious. We talked casually and more intimately about our lives. We connected. Flirted. Kissed. Then we kissed some more.

While I shower and get dressed in a simple pair of green shorts and a white tank top, I run through every scenario I can come up with to prepare for meeting JQ's mother and father.

Are they cold or are they cool—as in do they realize their son is an adult and is dating a woman and are okay with it?

But wait, are we officially dating?

My thoughts scramble and jam until I hear a knock at the

door. Hair wet and in my towel, I check through the side window. It's JQ. His back faces the door and he gazes at the fence that divides our properties.

Spinning in a circle, I'm afraid to answer it. What if he decided he doesn't want me to come with him to Texas? What will we do on the ride there? What if his parents hate me? How will they treat me when they discover I'm a washed-up musician?

JQ knocks again. I throw my hair into a pile on my head, smooth my shirt, and then open the door with a sunny, "Good morning."

"You okay?" he asks, instantly sensing my spiraling state.

"You okay?" I echo.

He smirks. "Yeah. I'm a little surprised by this turn of events, but I'm good. Cool." He leans in and adds, "Excited."

My breath is stilted when I exhale. "I thought you were coming over here to say that last night was a mistake and that I should pack up and ship out."

"What? No. Not at all." JQ plants his hands on my shoulders and his gaze drifts down before popping back up to my eyes. "Listen, I've never really done this before. It's new to me."

"*This* meaning us?" I wag my finger between us.

"This meaning everything that happened last night." He speaks slow and low.

Meanwhile, I'm in a frenzy. "Everything? Was I your first kiss?"

His eyes crinkle with a smile. "No, but it had been a while. What I mean is we went from hating each other to—"

"To sharing a meal, kissing, and dating," I say all in one breath.

JQ nods, confirming the *D* word. "All in one night. But I'm not worried about it. Don't regret it. I don't want you to either, unless—"

"No, I'm the *opposite* of whatever regret is." I bounce a little on my toes, unable to contain my relief.

"I know it was a little fast, but why don't we just take things as they come, manageable pieces? Little bites," he adds, referencing his comment last night.

"I like that."

He takes my hand in his, holds tight, and then says, "But you're not going to like this."

The little clouds under my feet disperse. "What do you mean?"

"Someone stole the giant root beer mug from the Tickle Chateau property." He pulls a green piece of paper out of his pocket and unfolds it.

The Pest Digest is a single sheet of legal paper folded in half and printed on both sides. It comes out every Sunday and has various sections related to the goings on in town. At the very bottom are some gardening tips. But in this special edition, across the banner head, is the announcement that the mug is missing.

"Who would do that?" I ask, scanning the article.

"Investigation pending per Deputy Lawson." JQ exhales. "But they think it was you."

"Who? Me? What? The authorities think I took it? It must weigh hundreds of pounds. How? Where? Why?"

JQ shakes his head. "Not the police, but the townspeople do. It's easy to blame the newcomer."

"But why would I steal it when I'm actively trying to get it back on the roof and restore the Penny Gamble to its previous glory?"

He looks over both his shoulders like the thick air itself in Hogwash is suspicious and says, "We should go inside."

The coffee is done percolating, and we both sit down at the

bistro table by the window. JQ drinks his black. I take mine light and sweet.

But the expression on his face is anything but. "Where to begin? Remember I told you about the pirate treasure and the Metairie Stronghold?"

"Yeah, it was an old fort."

"Supposedly, Hogan Tickle made a fortune in commodities and then invested in real estate, well, a town. Because why go home when you can go big and buy over twenty-five thousand acres?"

"I take it that became Hogwash Holler."

He nods. "The waterfront too."

"More like a swamp."

"That included the fort as well. Some people speculate it's because of the rumored treasure buried there. Others say Hogan found it and each of his buddies struck it rich with the—"

I snap my fingers, remembering the story JQ told me, "The Dubois Diamond, the Roger Cahoot Ruby, and the third one which was unknown."

"That's right. That was him and the Boot Boys, but it's all speculation."

"How exactly did Hogan Tickle get into making root beer?"

"Sassafras fields in abundance—an alternative to illegal beverages of that time is my guess. I'm not exactly sure. However, what I do know is that when Hogan died, he didn't leave that part of his fortune to his son."

"Did they have a falling out?"

"Another mystery. But he left the five riddles on his grave-stone. Many speculate they're clues to his inheritance. Count-less have tried to solve them, but as far as anyone knows, the supposed treasure is still out there, waiting to be found. That's all anyone knows, well, according to Cory."

Coffee forgotten, I lean in, captivated. "Why riddles do you suppose?"

He shrugs. "A bunch of nonsense if you ask me, but that doesn't stop people from buying into it. Cory would tell them to me and the guys in our platoon, but no one ever solved them, at least that I'm aware."

"Will you take me to the cemetery so I can take a picture before we leave?"

"Don't get too caught up in it. It's all just urban legend."

"You mean rural legends. But Cory must've thought they meant something if he told you all this. Please take me over there."

His expression remains flat.

"Pretty please?"

"You're not going to stop asking me about it until we go, huh?"

My lips widen with a grin. "Nope."

"Okay, come on."

We sneak out the back and cut behind houses and side roads. In less than five minutes we're at the town cemetery once more. Spanish moss drips from the oaks and if it were dusk instead of the brightest hours of the day, I'd be spooked even though we've been here once before. It's hard not to let curiosity get to me, probably as it did so many other treasure seekers who came to Hogwash.

We pass numerous gravestones, all above ground before we reach Hogan Tickle's massive mausoleum.

I take a picture with my phone, recalling the five riddles.

I would just as soon imbibe this root as take to the air and make a hoot. Look up and see me on the blocks the blocks made of pinkish rocks. You'll find me sketched there, most rectangular seldom square.

"The guy sure had an interesting sense of humor," I whisper, feeling like that's the right volume in a cemetery. There will be no hooting here.

JQ reads the next one, "'Take one from apple but none from tart. Find one in liver but not in heart. The last you'll discover in giant as well as ghost but never, ever in a roast.'"

"Let's not talk about ghosts right now," I whisper then read the next one in my head.

I have a head and a tail. I can break, but I am not frail. If you feed me, I will plink, but don't you worry, I do not stink.

JQ's smize appears when I trace my finger over the word *cuddle* in the third riddle. We sure got cozy last night.

You can hold me tight but not to cuddle. However, I prefer the muddle minus three especially if there's a puddle. I cannot sew or sow, but I am the latter and getting fatter.

"This one kind of reminds me of the story of the Three Little Pigs: 'The story is that of the three, one lives in a house made of a tree. The other you could blow over, but not mine even though it's in a field of clover.'"

JQ lets out a long breath. "Most people agree that these are the first clues in the scavenger hunt that leads to the five golden tokens which people believe leads to the ruby and whatever else Hogan had squirreled away."

"I take it no one ever found the Golden Tokens?"

"Nope, but many have looked. As I understand it, Hogan did leave some property rights to members of his family, but not the shiny stuff. Not the fortune."

"The treasure."

"If he even had it in the first place. Could've been a story the guy told to entertain himself. According to Cory, who heard stories from Nan, the old man was odd, unique, inclined to tell whoppers."

A morbid thought crosses my mind. "But if he didn't leave the riddle teasing the tokens until after he died, what would it matter? It's not like his ghost is lingering around town, laughing at everyone racing around on the hunt."

JQ shrugs. "This is Hogwash, Lexi."

Hope flashes inside. "But what if it's not?"

"Not Hogwash?"

"The other definition of hogwash. Nonsense."

"Said everyone who ever searched and came up empty-handed after turning this town over and inside out. Lexi, no one has ever found one of the tokens. There's a good chance the whole thing was made up or the tokens are buried in the bayou. Lost forever."

I slowly shake my head as a small golden coin takes shape in my mind and then drops into a fountain like a wish.

JQ continues, "Hogan died in 1963 and less than a year later, fortune seekers started showing up in Hogwash. It began a cottage industry, including hotels and restaurants to host the visitors along with the various attractions. The economy was strong until his son died in 1989. Some say that sent a curse over the area. Others speculate that there was never a treasure and the old man is laughing in his grave."

"What do you think?"

JQ leans back and crosses his hands over his chest as though he hasn't given it much thought. "I think we all have to make our own way and relying on other people to share their treasure is going to leave you wanting and waiting for a long time."

"I agree. But Dirk and Suzie Lou do not," I mutter.

He nods. "And if you get a bonus in life like a ruby, then that's like the cherry on top of the sundae."

"But you said treasure seekers were searching for years. You might argue that if they found it, they earned it in a way."

"I suppose if they applied themselves to the task, but most people came to town, did a rubbing of the grave, half-heartedly tried to solve the riddle, and then dug holes in any level ground that wasn't swamp."

"So, it was *buried* treasure?"

JQ shrugs. "No one knows beyond what the riddles say."

"So, anything that was Hogan Tickle's might be a clue...including the giant crystal mug of root beer?" I ask, taking a guess.

"Hadn't thought of that, but I suppose so."

"Up until now, I didn't know anything about the scavenger hunt and I have an alibi." I wink.

"I am your witness, but I ordered some security cameras for the Penny Gamble. I'll set them up while you pack, and then we can hit the road. Probably good to get out of town until this blows over."

JQ walks me to my house and I can't decide if I'm more nervous about meeting his parents or being implicated in a crime by the town busybodies.

Chapter 18

The Golden Tickle

Not going to lie, the idea that someone has targeted The Penny Gamble *and* Lexi tans my hide. I don't like it. Won't abide by it.

After setting up a video surveillance system and connecting the app to my phone, I inspect every window, door, and access point. With everything secure, I'm ready to hit the road when Lexi comes in, backlit and pure sunshine in a sundress, her hair a cute mess piled on her head and biting the bottom of her plush lip.

"JQ, I've been thinking about something," she starts.

My stomach drops. Maybe she's having second thoughts about coming to my parents' with me. It's a big step. A quick step. But we Texas boys are known to do that—the two-step that is. The other part, the falling and meeting the parents bit is brand new to me, but I'm not the kind of person to think twice. I was trained to evaluate and execute. To make decisions and follow through.

Bracing myself, I ask, "What's on your mind?"

She lets out a shaky breath. "I thought I saw something."

I lean in, not expecting her to say that. More like, *My bags aren't packed. I think we're moving too fast, so I'm staying here this weekend.* In which case, I would've dropped everything because I won't let her face the rootbeer burglary alone.

"Something suspicious?" I ask, my mind honing in on the saboteur and thief.

"More like curious." She tentatively crosses the room, passing the jukebox, and stopping in front of the brick wall.

"You want to fire this old thing up?" I guess. Wearing a little smile, I flick the switch. "I was going to surprise you when we got back, but Nat Grandworth was able to tune it up."

Lexi steps back as the neon gas fills the old tubes of the jukebox, making it glow before reaching the pig, which illuminates in a soft pink with gold wings.

Her eyes bright, she says, "Wow. This is amazing. I can't believe it works."

"It's a classic. All the old EPs, the records, inside were fully intact even though Nat said it hadn't turned on in years."

Lexi bounces a little on her toes. "This is exciting. Gives me hope for the grand opening. What song should we play first?" She browses the oldies on the list and clicks a button, but nothing happens.

"Oh, we need one of these." I dig into my pocket and retrieve a quarter.

When it drops into the machine, the opening strains of an old song echo through the space before a male voice belts out a familiar song called "Only You," by the Platters.

Lexi beams a smile, marveling at the ancient technology. It's a slow song and before I realize what's happening, her hands are in mine and we're dancing.

Her eyes sparkle and she tips her head back with laughter.

"What's so funny?"

"You can dance."

"We're kind of swaying from side to side." But my smirk grows. "But yes, I can dance. It comes with the territory."

"What do you mean?" Lexi asks.

"Are you still coming with me to Texas?"

"Of course. I don't want the Hoggers coming at me." Then her shoulder jostles. "And I've never done the whole 'meet the parents thing.' It seems like a pretty big deal. One I wouldn't pass up."

I can't help but wonder what that means for us, that she too knows it's not a nothing burger—my mouth waters because my father is the grill king. No doubt we'll be having burgers from our homegrown cattle. Mom treats them like a pasture full of princesses.

Our eyes meet briefly like we both realize something big is happening between us and when the song ends, our hands don't drop. I don't expect they'll be separate for long on the ride west.

Recalling what Lexi originally said when she found me in here, I ask, "So what were you curious about?"

"I have a confession." She lets go of my hand and wrings hers together. "Remember the night you came home late and thought you saw someone in here?"

My body turns icy.

"That was me."

"What do you mean?" The ice thaws my thoughts, sending them pinging around like a pinball machine—which would be a cool thing to have in here. Is Lexi trying to sabotage our efforts? Collect insurance money?

"I thought I heard something and was kind of spooked, so I snuck down with a sheet. I wore it over my head like a ghost and—"

It cannot be helped. I belt out a laugh from deep in my stomach. I could be mad, but no, this is hilarious.

"So you weren't wrong. It was me, but I felt foolish and then totally embarrassed myself the next morning." She bites her lip again. "I didn't exactly realize it entirely then, but I guess I kind of sort of cared what you thought of me."

"Is that another way to say that you liked me?"

"Like is a strong word."

I chuckle again—it's part relief and part amusement at this woman who broke down and broke into my life. "Was that all?"

"Actually, no."

"There's more?" I grip the counter, wondering what it could possibly be.

"As I said, I thought I saw something." She draws a chair next to the jukebox and then steps onto it, hands pawing the brick wall.

"Lexi, be careful. What are you doing?"

"It glinted in your headlights."

"It was late and you were prowling with a sheet over your head," I say, dismissing it because we really should get on the road.

"Ah ha. Right here. See?" She makes a giddy sound.

I lift onto my toes, squinting, I do see the edge of something shiny, but it's probably metal, reinforcing the brick wall.

Lexi picks at the brick's mortar with her fingernail. Quickly realizing that we're not going anywhere until she digs it out, I look around for a sharp tool. From the other side of the room, I glimpse her perched up there, legs long, arms extended. It's an odd but beautiful sight and more than anything, I want to see it every day. See Lexi every day, though preferably on solid ground.

And that's what she's given me these last weeks—solid ground, an anchor, even though she's the most whimsical and playful person I've ever met. The cool thing is she knows herself and knows what she's about.

"JQ, I think it's—"

At the same time, I gasp. "Lexi, get down."

Alarmed, she ducks as if seeking cover. "Are the Hoggers after me?"

"Come here." Urgency fills my voice.

"Are the townsfolk coming with flaming torches and pitch-forks, ready to drive me out?"

A soft chuckle escapes, but I can hardly believe my eyes. I grip Lexi by the shoulders and position her in front of me but facing the wall where she'd been standing on the chair.

"Do you see it?" I point.

She tilts her head to the side. "The brick wall?"

"The mortar between the bricks. The faint lines. The flying pig."

She squints at the pinkish bricks.

I whisper, "I would just as soon imbibe this root as take to the air and make a hoot. Look up and see me on the blocks, the blocks made of pinkish rocks. You'll find me sketched there, most rectangular seldom square."

Lexi's gasp matches mine from moments before. "And that shiny thing is the eye of a flying pig. That's the answer to the riddle." She runs toward the chair and the shiny object wedged in the mortar.

I see exactly what she means. "It looks like it's winking."

We both laugh and then scramble around to find a ladder.

After a more careful inspection, the shiny object is a circular disk in the shape of a coin, or a token. I can only see the edge but it's relatively smooth and has hammered edges.

I manage to chip away at the mortar and climb down with it safely in my hand. I open my palm.

Lexi looks from it to me and then at it again. "I think that's a token, JQ."

"I think you're right."

"But what do we do with it?"

I shrug. "I'd imagine it would come with instructions like a scavenger hunt. Maybe finding the coin was the prize in and of itself. It looks like real gold to me."

Lexi takes it in her hand and examines it. On the front is a stamp of a flying pig with an engraving that looks like a year. "What does MDCCCXC mean?"

"Are you sure that's what it says? Could be a code or Roman numerals. Let's see, *M* denotes one thousand. If I remember correctly *D* is five hundred. *C* denotes one hundred. *X* is ten but two *X*s are twenty and the three *I*s are three. So that would be one thousand, five hundred plus three one hundreds and—" I scratch my temple. "Actually, it could be a year. 1890?"

"Anything significant happen during that year?"

"I'd have to refer to an encyclopedia."

Lexi flips the coin over. "On this side is merely the letter I."

"Or Roman numeral one, meaning we found Tickle's first Golden Token."

Our gazes lock. I gaze into Lexi's dark blue eyes.

"We found it and we weren't even looking," she whispers.

But the real treasure is that I found her, but there is something to be said about finding what you seek when you stop striving so hard—not that I was looking for love. There's probably some sage wisdom in there about getting what you need when you're actively in search of the opposite: solitude, the solvable puzzle of metal engines and components, and merely the companionship of man's best friend—Peaches is probably wondering what happened to us in here.

"Now what?" Lexi asks.

I scrub my hand along my jaw. "All things considered, with you being root beer mug public enemy number one, let's keep it between us for now."

"Good point." Lexi gazes at the coin and then at me. "When pigs fly." In a few short strides, she stands in front of the jukebox.

We both look from the coin to the glowing pink pig on top of the machine.

"Do you think—?" she asks.

I'm not sure what to think about aside from the woman beside me, holding her in my arms as we danced, and that we're supposed to be on our way to meet my parents.

"You could try."

She bites her lip, fingers pinching the coin, and hovering over the slot. "Worst case, we open up the jukebox and retrieve the coin. It's not like the machine could eat it." She turns to me then closes her eyes and slides the coin into the slot with a strong inhale.

A song I've never before heard comes out of the jukebox when Lexi exhales. It's a woman's voice, singing about discovering love on the bayou.

Lexi's eyes turn liquid and she smiles. "It's beautiful."

While she's likely appreciating the woman's voice, I'm carefully listening to the lyrics, searching for clues. Then again, perhaps Hogan's treasure was this song. Mine is the songstress in front of me.

When the music goes quiet, I say, "Funny that so often people think of treasure as diamonds, rubies, and gold."

Lexi fits her hand into mine. "I know what you mean. We should get going."

"So, you think that's it?" I ask, surprised that she's ready to give up the search.

"For now. We have parents to visit, remember?"

Yep, Lexi is my number one treasure because she just proved that she isn't in this for the money and that's more than enough for me.

Chapter 19

Running into the Storm

LEXI

P eaches is as pleased as punch to take the drive and rides in my lap the whole way to a little town short of Houston. Time flies by like, well, like a flying pig as we speculate about the riddle, the coin, and the song.

The woman's voice was deep and soulful yet velvety like a pleasantly warm night—the kind with fireflies, the soft lapping of waves, and a kiss in the moonlight. Well, those were the lyrics. Ones I'll never forget. We tried to match it with the songs listed on the jukebox, but we knew them all—classic oldies and deduced it was a hidden track.

I also can't help but think about slow dancing with JQ, the way his eyes seem to soak me in, how he listens so carefully, warms me so fully. Forget the golden bean juice, I found my golden token and it's a man with broad shoulders, brown eyes that smile for me and me alone, and who smells like engine grease mixed with the manly scent of clove and spice.

Once in Texas, we drive down a rambling, dirt road with cows on one side and the occasional break in the line of pines and palms with a gate, indicating a ranch.

We reach one with an iron gate with the letter *W*, presumably for JQ's last name, Ward, in a circle across the front. He pulls slowly down a paved driveway with two horses grazing to the right and a mixture of brown and black cows munching grass on the left.

JQ pulls to a stop in front of a big ranch home with pale yellow paint and white trim. The grand entry porch bordered by large windows is the stuff rocking chair dreams are made of.

"You grew up out here? It's beautiful."

"And quiet."

I take that to mean no gossip. Honey called on the way here and asked how I'm holding up. Because JQ was driving, I told her myself and we traded phone numbers as well. The truth is, I'm fine, well, I was until we got here and the reality of meeting Mr. and Mrs. Ward hit me full steam.

JQ reaches for my hand. "They are going to love you and not in the southern *Bless your heart* kind of way when they really mean something else. Seriously, you have no idea how happy my mom is going to be."

"Does she know you brought a friend?"

JQ squeezes my hand. "She knows I brought my girlfriend."

"So, we're doing this?" I ask.

"I never hated you, Lexi. I was wary, sure. Taken by surprise, definitely. Immature, yes. But—" He tilts his head and gazes at me. His eyes are two big grins. "I've never felt this way, and that's saying a lot because I'm not a feely kind of guy."

When I open the door, Peaches bounds out of the car. The garage is on the side of the house and she runs in that direction. I notice more than a few cars parked over there—four big trucks, an assortment of vintage vehicles that remind of me the Duster, and a sporty SUV.

Before I can chase after the dog, JQ reaches for my hand.

"She'll be fine. She knows her way around here and is probably looking for Buster. Though looking is relative. More like sniffing."

JQ puts me at ease in time for the front door to open and a woman with thick brown curls to her shoulders, a pink button-down shirt, and cowgirl boots glides toward us. She greets us with warm hellos and he makes introductions.

Mrs. Ward pulls me into a hug like we're already family. Not going to lie, she's a really good hugger. I might be mistaken, but I'm pretty sure she whispers, "Thank you," into my ear. Though Peaches found Buster and they're yipping happily in the yard, so it's hard to hear.

JQ claps his hand lightly. "Okay, Mom. You can let Lexi go now. No strangleholds."

He must see my eyes widen.

"I'm just happy to meet you. I've heard so much about you." Mrs. Ward grips my hand.

I tilt my head in question.

JQ's ears tint. "We chatted last night."

She winks at me. "Come on in. The gang is here and is excited to meet you too."

"Mom," JQ hisses. "I said not to make a fuss."

"What kind of Texan would I be if I didn't make a fuss?" She goes on to list all the food she fixed and we bond over the Sm'ookie. Ten minutes later, I've met more Ritchies than I can keep track of. And it turns out this is only a tenth of the extended family and does not include JQ's dad's side.

"Next time, you'll have to come out to the ranch," Parker says.

"Lexi would love that. She's a songwriter and singer, you know." JQ beams.

I wave my hand dismissively. "It's nothing. I'm now the

proud part-owner of the Penny Gamble. Those days are behind me."

"Not if I have any say in it." JQ continues, "Lexi wrote a song and her ex-boyfriend stole it and gave it to her rival."

"That sounds like a song in and of itself," Jamison says.

"Don't tell me it's *I'd Run into the Storm for You* by Suzie Lou?" Duke asks.

JQ aims finger guns at his cousin and then puts on the CD that Nan gave him. Everyone is quiet as they listen. A couple of people tap their boots on the floor. Others nod along. Mrs. Ward smiles like all of her prayers have been answered. Mr. Ward wraps his arm around his wife as if the lyrics speak to them.

When it ends, Duke says, "I have an ear for that kind of thing. I knew that wasn't that girl's song. Now, plenty of singers have writers behind them, and there's no shame in that. But right from the jump, there was something about that hit that felt off to me." Hunter glowers.

"Well, it still became a hit." I shrug.

"And I bet you have more in you," Shawnee says.

I appreciate JQ's enthusiasm and support, but I don't know what the future holds. If it's a tossup between us and my career, I'm afraid of both options.

After snacks and a tour of the property, JQ's brother arrives just as his cousins inform us they have to head out.

"We have a three-hour drive and want to stay ahead of that storm," Tucker says.

They say a long goodbye, leaving me to think about the future, but before I crawl too deep into my thoughts, someone taps me on the shoulder.

"You make sure you come up to Ritchie Ranch at some point, we could have a session, and show off your voice to the rest of the family," Duke says.

I tilt my head, slowly making a connection. "You said Ritchie Ranch, as in the Ritchies as in the C.o.w.b.o.y.s. the famous band?"

"You got it. Didn't JQ tell you?" Shawnee says.

"No, he did not mention that he's related to Duke or Lucy or any of them," I say, raising my voice loud enough for him to hear.

He frowns. "Could've sworn I'd mentioned it."

"I'm pretty sure I would recall you casually commenting that you're related to some of the most acclaimed country musicians in the world." I nod my head. "Yeah, that would've stuck in my mind."

JQ's eyes crinkle as if he's pleased with himself for how happy this makes me even though I'm giving him a hard time—and doing my best to play it cool because I am so fangirling right now. The Ritchies heard me singing the original version of *I'd Run into the Storm for You*. And maybe in the long run that matters more than Dirk and Suzie Lou.

After waving goodbye, we head inside and I help get dinner ready while JQ and his dad go check on the animals and batten down the hatches for the incoming weather.

Mrs. Ward and I talk about everything from food to soda fountains to meeting JQ for the first time.

A deep male voice says, "I bet you hated him at first."

I spin around, but instead of JQ, as I expect, it's his brother, John. He's slightly shorter and his hair is slightly lighter. Oh, and he smiles easily, but otherwise, they're nearly identical. Same broad shoulders, muscles, and tattoos.

Mrs. Ward leans in, waiting for my answer.

"Well, he didn't make it easy to like him."

John snaps his fingers. "I knew it. I was with him out in the barn for all of thirty minutes, and he's a changed man. Tell us, what kind of magic did you work?"

"She makes a great Sm'ookie," Mrs. Ward says, cutting John a piece.

"Lived here for eighteen years and had to eat dinner before dessert. Grow up, move out, and the woman is giving me sweets before we sit down. Make it make sense."

We all laugh.

"Just wait until I have grandkids. They will be so spoiled," Mrs. Ward says.

They both look at me. "Yes, I want kids."

Again, they laugh.

John plonks down on a kitchen stool and takes a sip of root beer, reminding me that I'm potentially wanted in another state for stealing a giant, revolving root beer mug.

"So what do you want to know about my bro?"

"JP, no telling my girlfriend that I cried on the playground when you pushed me off the monkey bars. I was five." JQ, smelling like hay, kisses me on the cheek and then gives one to his mom on the cheek while snagging a carrot from the counter and taking a bite.

"Wait, you're JP and you're JQ?"

JP presses his hand to his chest. "John Pace Ward. It's a pleasure to meet you. Your surprise suggests you don't know your boyfriend's full name."

JQ rolls his eyes.

"It's a family name," Mrs. Ward says as if they've had this conversation before.

"Tell her," JP teases.

JQ huffs then says, "My full-given name is Jacques Quill Ward."

My grin grows. "I like it."

"Well, the kids on that same playground thought Jacques was funny."

"So, he went by JQ," Mrs. Ward says.

"I say you should've gone with Jake."

"There was already a Jake in my class."

"I think it's a wonderful name. It was your grandfather's." Mrs. Ward goes on to say that John, Pace, Jacques, and Quill were hers and Mr. Ward's respective grandfathers' names.

"I agree with Mrs. Ward. I like both names and would consider carrying on the tradition."

JQ coughs on his carrot.

John pats him roughly on the back.

Mrs. Ward and I exchange a smile.

After dinner, we sit on the back porch while Mrs. Ward gets dessert ready. Mr. Ward and JQ chat about the ranch, leaving John to tell me stories about his brother.

"What else should I know?" Questions about the Golden Token and the song on the jukebox try to jump to the front of the line. I can't help my curiosity.

"I can help with that," John says.

"Don't you dare," JQ says as if he'd been keeping an ear on our conversation.

Disregarding his brother, John says, "JQ is a Navy SEAL and I'm a Green Beret. We try to out-Captain America each other. But I can tell he likes you. A lot."

And I like him too. Maybe more than like.

After banana Foster pie for dessert, we play a rousing board game that reminds me of charades. John and I team up and Mr. & Mrs. Ward are a pair, leaving JQ with Peaches. The guy with the dog wins. He's certainly won my heart.

I thank the Wards and catch John flashing his brother a gesture that says he has his eyes on him while we all say goodnight.

After everyone heads up, JQ, Peaches, and I remain at the foot of the stairs. We make a fuss petting her and giving her good belly rubs before bed. Truth is, like last night, I don't exactly want this one to end. At least not until I get a kiss.

Before I get back to my feet, Peaches distracts me and I go all in on the baby dog talk. JQ too.

"Who's a good girl?" I ask.

"Who's the best girl?" JQ says.

"Who sat on my lap and got treats the whole drive here?"

"Who runs around like a wild puppy beast? It's Peaches. Yes, it is."

"I love you. Yes, I do," I say, giving her rump one last pet.

"I love you too," JQ says.

The dog is in hog heaven, but her owner abruptly stands up, mumbles, "Good night," and then rushes upstairs.

Peaches bounds after him and streaks down the hall just before his bedroom door closes. I blink a few times, confused. It isn't until I'm in the shower, replaying the strange scene, wondering if JQ had to go to the bathroom, forgot to shut off a device, or something else, that I realize what happened.

I said, *I love you.*

He said, *I love you too.*

I swallow thickly as I get out of the shower. The first crack of thunder from that storm shakes the house.

JQ told me he loved me, but then he spooked.

Chapter 20

Into Your Arms Forever

LEXI

Along hour passes while I lay in bed, rehashing the brief exchange at the foot of the stairs with Peaches as our surrogate, the bearer of our *I love yous*.

Yes, I was talking to the dog, but I love JQ too. I realized it the other day. Thought about it seriously yesterday, and fully experienced it today. I love that man and his dog and his family.

Tossing and turning, my thoughts tune to static and my heart squeezes because either he said that by accident, said it and realized he didn't feel it, or said it and is terrified. Either way, like the saboteur at the Penny Gamble, he'll ruin this for us.

Given the fact that I wasn't JQ's first kiss, but the first person he's brought home, his track record with romance doesn't look too good.

It's also hard not to think about the moment we shared in the Penny Gamble, the dance, the token, and the song that played on the jukebox. The lyrics come to me now in snippets.

Along the shore, you walked alone. Until I saw you were the one. Sights set high, you didn't let me down.

But JQ has. Whoever the singer was and whoever she was in love with, must've gotten their happily ever after. Now, I get to be a hopeless romantic, in a literal way. My hope for romance has diminished and is fading fast.

The static gets louder, and like tuning a radio dial, I try to make sense of it, and understand what happened and where he's coming from. Instead of the contents of our conversation, other words come to me. Lyrical ones.

I run through them in my mind a few times and the static turns into a melody. I bolt upright in bed. The creative block is gone. I scramble across the room to my purse for the notebook I always carry with me when voices filter from outside on the L-bend of the back porch.

Lightning brightens the room for a moment, and I recognize the silhouette of JQ and the nearly identical one of JP.

I'd close the window if it weren't sweltering. I don't mean to listen but can't help but hear JP say, "She brings out the happy in you."

"I've been thinking of moving up north."

"To the place with the pizza and pie that you're always raving about?" JP asks.

"It's really good."

"What about the woman you love? What about that Sm'ookie she makes?"

I don't hear JQ's response over another crack of thunder and I'm afraid to, so I slam the window shut and hurry to bed.

Not surprisingly, the next morning, JQ is distant. It's like the storm blew away whatever feelings he had for me. His parents are busy around the property but left quiche for breakfast. He stares into his empty cup of coffee.

I try to tease, "I told you my name is Lexington and you failed to mention you're Jacques Quill."

"There's a lot you don't know about me, Lexi."

"But I'm enjoying getting to know those things."

"I should go help Dad with the animals."

I don't hide my frown, but he exits without looking back.

Not a minute later, John enters the kitchen. "I'd like to blame my brother's bad behavior on his not being a morning person. But—"

"But he told you what happened last night with Peaches?"

John nods. "He also told me that—" He shakes his head. "That's a conversation for you to have with him. But what you need to know is that JQ took it hard after Cory died. He went nose to the grindstone in the military. He has more awards and commendations than most. And trust me, we've been competing for years."

"Oh, right, the fight for Captain America's shield." I mean for the words to sound light, funny but they land with a thud.

"The only thing JQ knows how to do is fight."

"Yeah, we went at it when we first met."

"A couple of years ago, he got wounded. Took a desk job. Most guys don't want that and would rather have the glory of the field, but he said if it meant he could keep serving his country, he'd do it. However, I think it was because he didn't want to face the things he'd been running from. Namely Cory's death. Sitting at that desk gave him plenty of time to think though. Either that or Nan's declining health prompted him to take the medical retirement offer. He went to Hogwash to nurse his wounds."

"You sure they weren't self-inflicted?"

John tips his head from side to side. "And that's why he... Lexi, he pushed you away because he's afraid to get close to anyone. Hidden under the tough exterior is a good guy. A great one."

"I know that, but are you sure you don't mean a jawbreaker candy?"

"That's the hard candy shell. But really, beneath is a guy with emotions he doesn't know what to do with. He's processed Cory's death but hasn't figured out how to move forward. That's where you come in."

The truth is, I like JQ and I think he likes me, but neither one of us is ready, so we pretended to hate each other to keep the other at arm's distance. But now what? What happens now that we like each other?

I spend the better part of the morning with Mrs. Ward before she loads us up with leftovers and makes me promise to come back. If she sensed things between JQ and me cooled off, she didn't mention it.

John gives JQ the same two-finger, *I have my eyes on you* gesture as he did last night.

Once in the truck, Peaches reclaims her spot in my lap, but suffice it to say, the ride back is long, quiet, and awkward.

JQ pulls into the short driveway between The Penny Gamble Soda Fountain and Cory's Automotive Service Station. He remains quiet. So I guess that's it. As quickly as it started, it's over.

This might be my last chance, so why not go out with a bang? I blurt, "That was nice until last night. Thanks for freaking out. I mean, thanks for the ride back."

JQ winces.

Peaches whines as I exit the truck.

This time, I don't look back.

I consider gassing up Dusty and hitting the road, but no sooner do I close the door, and the first tear falls, the last line from the song on the jukebox floats into my mind in a deep and velvety voice.

The woman had been singing about meeting a man and falling for him.

Along the shore, you walked alone. Until I saw you were the one. Sights set high, you didn't let me down.

She described them dancing in the sassafrass field, but not just in poetic, flowery language.

From the dock, you took two steps north and didn't leave me behind. I followed your lead three and twenty combined. In the middle, our love came true, and you have my word that I'll never leave you blue.

I can't help but think it sounds like she was giving directions, like a treasure map. Either that or I don't want to think about how JQ has left me blue.

But those weren't the last lines. They were, *You know where to find me. I'll always be there. My love buried deep in the wooden square.*

If things aren't going to work out between JQ and me, there's no way I can stay in Hogwash. And if there is buried treasure, it wouldn't hurt to get a little headstart on a new life far away from here.

I have no idea where the sassafrass fields are and before I can consult a map, someone knocks. Instead of the welcome wagon, it's probably the paddy wagon this time, ready to cart me off for supposedly stealing the root beer mug. I have my alibi at the ready even if JQ probably thinks it was a mistake bringing me to meet his parents.

However, instead of the police, it's JQ and Peaches. "Will you come next door for a minute?"

I'm afraid the saboteur struck again.

"Actually, while you're here, do you have any idea where the sassafras fields are?"

"Sure, out past Daley's sweet potato farm. Why?"

I sing the song from the jukebox. For half a minute, JQ's eyes glaze over as if he's hypnotized. He must be tired.

"I know it was a long drive, but could you take me out there real quick? I promise you don't even have to say a word to me. Just pretend I'm not there."

JQ opens his mouth.

I cut him off. "Please, just this one favor, and then I'll be out of your hair for good."

He lets out a breath and closes his eyes. "Sure."

The ride is quiet and bumpy. Clouds roll in, dark and ominous. I do my best to remember the rest of the song, hoping it'll provide clues.

When we reach the land, I spot a creek but no dock. Whereas I expect something similar to a field of cotton or tubers, instead, it's a grove of trees. They have mitten-shaped leaves and are relatively low to the ground compared to the pines in the distance.

"I was expecting something more like grass," I admit.

"Rhymes with sassafras," JQ says.

Seated between us, Peaches looks from him to me and back again.

"Do you mind if I look around? There was a shore and a dock mentioned in the song."

"There's a creek over that way." JQ points as if he has no intention of getting out.

I open the door and hop down. With an excited bark, Peaches follows me, which means JQ joins us too, but with heavy, begrudging footfalls.

The lyrics to the song play on repeat in my mind, but it was an old tune, old enough to be in the jukebox, so whatever the woman sang about is likely long gone and perhaps the sassafras trees were saplings at the time, meaning this could've been a field.

I wander around and nothing turns up or lights my curiosity. Hopelessness trails me. I spot JQ by the creek and call for him, to let him know we can leave. But he remains still, unmoving.

Peaches frolics along the shoreline of a creek. He runs his thumb over something at hip height.

"We can—" I'm about to add *leave* when he interrupts.

"I found something." Under his fingers, carved into the wooden pole of a dilapidated dock, are the letters PG + HT.

"Hogan Tickle?" I guess.

"PG? Penny Gamble?" he asks.

I turn in a circle, following her voice. *"From the dock, you took two steps north and didn't leave me behind. I followed your lead three and twenty combined. In the middle, our love came true, and you have my word that I'll never leave you blue."*

"You have a beautiful voice, Lexi," JQ says.

I didn't even realize I was singing.

His tone is as heavy as his steps, plodding behind me. Peaches scampers ahead, nose to the ground as if she realizes we're hunting for something.

But it's okay if we don't discover the treasure. I found JQ, even if briefly. I got to experience the sparks of love.

He stops next to a tree in a clearing as if also realizing it's pointless...and anything between us is hopeless.

"Look, the initials are carved here again," he says.

Peaches barks excitedly then goes quiet when thunder claps in the distance.

I glance up, down, and all around. JQ does the same.

"You know where to find me. I'll always be there. My love buried deep in the wooden square."

"Buried?" JQ repeats.

"Do you have a shovel in your truck?" I ask.

The corner of his lip lifts like maybe this isn't a wild goose chase after all. Peaches chases him back to the truck and they return in two minutes.

"Where do we dig? There's so much ground. The square

could be anywhere." My gaze darts all over and then lands on JQ.

He looks at the trees in the clearing and then, eyes bright, back to me as if remembering we make good partners. "There are four. They form a *square* and if you draw a line between them," he does so with the shovel, "the X marks the spot."

I gasp, and he plunges the shovel into the ground. Peaches helps with her claws. I wish I had a tool to help. However, in five minutes, the shovel hits something hard.

Smoothing away the dirt, the top of a box, a square, takes shape. My pulse pounding, we dig it out. The box isn't a treasure chest so much as an ammunition storage container with a flat handle on the top.

"My guess is this dates back to World War II," JQ says.

"Should we open it?" Lightning cracking the sky answers the question.

He lets out a breath and then says, "If we do, there's no going back. People will find out."

"Do they have to? I mean, it depends on what's inside."

"It's heavy. Very heavy." JQ strains as he tries to pull it out of the hole.

I wrap my arms around his waist from behind and tug on him as he pulls on the container. For half a second, I want to melt into him—his solid frame, strength, and comforting warmth.

Instead, we both groan as we jerk the box out of the ground, sending us spilling backward. Our bodies tangle and with it my feelings for him. I don't want to give up on us. The twisty tingles rush through me when our gazes meet. His eyes are all smiles like it hits him that we're out here in the middle of a grove with a box full of something and a dog yelping excitedly, running in circles like it contains treats. I sense something shift ever so slightly as if he realizes there's no getting rid of me now...and maybe he doesn't want to.

"Okay, you ready for this?" JQ asks.

I sense he's asking himself as much as me. Is he ready to let the past go and move forward? Am I part of that?

"Whatever comes, let's do it." I mean for excitement to fill my tone. Instead, it's pure confidence, like a general leading the charge. Only, instead of being on opposite sides, now we're fighting for each other.

With a nod, JQ opens the box. On the top is an envelope and beneath that glows a shiny bar of gold.

"Lots of bars. They're very gold," I whisper.

"And the letter."

A fat plop of rain lands on my nose.

"We should head back."

Together, we carry the box with the letter tucked safely inside. We're both quiet on the ride like the gravity of what we discovered draws our mouths closed, but the storm moves off, leaving the sky clear when we get back to town.

Parked in his driveway, I follow JQ to his backyard. He sits down in the same place he was when we kissed. The other chair is damp from the storm, so I have no choice but to join him. Our knees knock as I lower to sitting. I'd much rather keep my distance while he tears the rest of my heart in half, but here we are.

The box is on the ground by our feet along with Peaches who munches on a treat. JQ holds the letter lightly in his hand.

"Should we read it?" I ask, nodding.

JQ opens the envelope flap.

"Careful."

He passes it to me. "You should be the one to read it."

I take the paper. It's old, brittle, and yellow. "How about we do it together." Shimmying closer, I position it so we can both read the note, written to Hogan. It's quickly clear that it's a love letter from one sweetheart to another.

"From Penny to Hogan," JQ says.

"To Hogan, love Penny," I say.

"So the Penny Gamble..."

"Is named after his beloved?" I finish.

"From what we read, they must've been corresponding while he was away at war."

"I'm guessing his famous rootbeer recipe was from her." The postscript contains it, so maybe she was hoping he could get his hands on some sassafras while abroad. Maybe give him a little comfort of home.

"Look here, there are some Roman numerals." JQ points to the upper right-hand corner.

"Do you think it could've been a code they shared? Maybe MDCCCXC meant I love you."

"Or if Hogan was in the war, given his age," he does the calculation, "likely he was born around 1890, which would make sense."

"Ever practical. But I like the love note code theory."

The corner of JQ's mouth lifts and he knocks into me with his shoulder.

"They loved each other and she loved him enough to write a song for him. That's even better than secret code," I say.

"And he left some of his fortune buried in the square." JQ wears a smile and then lets out a breath. "I'm sorry."

"Me too. I understand. It's going to be hard to try to be partners after this. I can sell you my half of the Penny Gamble, if you want. I'll find something to do. Somewhere to go."

"No, I'm sorry, Lexington. I'm sorry that I let the past dictate the future I want with you." The way he says my name suggests this conversation is going in a different direction than I expected and at a much faster pace—then again, that's how we do things. "I'm sorry that my fears and ego got in the way last night."

I straighten. "Oh. I thought—"

"No regrets. You're the next chapter in my life, but I didn't know how to turn the page. Then while you were petting the dog and I said that," he clears his throat.

Peaches sits proudly by his side as if I have her to thank for bringing us back together. And Nan had a little something to do with it too.

"I said I love you too." He takes my hands and meets my eyes. "It's true. I love you, Lexi Dunn. This has all happened fast, but I think it was simmering since the moment we met. I saw you with your hair on top of your head and those sexy sunglasses, and that halter sundress on the side of the road... I knew that you'd mark the end of the man I was."

"I like the man you are."

"No, you like the man I've become. In this short time, you've made me better. I hope I've—"

And that's all JQ needs to say before I throw myself into his arms and press my mouth to his, sealing this moment, accepting his apology, making him mine.

When we part, I say, "You restored my hope. I used to be a hopeful romantic. You gave that back to me. I love you, JQ."

He holds my gaze. "I love you too."

Peaches lets out a little whine. JQ gives me an award-winning smize, and we both turn to her, full doggy baby talk, praising and petting our furry little matchmaker.

Epilogue

The summer is almost over even though it's still hot, sticky, and sunny. Honey bounces the baby on her hip while we stand in the short driveway between the soda fountain and Cory's shop where she found me just after I hung a new sign that says, *Gran Opening*. Yes, it's another This & That discount find.

"If I changed the *GR* to an *N*, it would say Nan Opening," I joke.

"She'd have liked that."

"Why's it called the Penny Gamble anyway?"

"Some say Hogan Tickle started the place with a mere penny in his pocket, meaning he took a gamble on whether it and the root beer would succeed. Others suggest he may have stayed on the right side of the law during prohibition by creating root beer instead of smuggling boot beer, having parted ways with the Boot Beer Boys." She winks.

"But that's not what you think," I say, taking a guess. As it is, I have a theory of my own.

"I'm not entirely sure he kept his side of the street clean.

Word is he liked to gamble. Maybe it's a reference or perhaps—"

Before she can finish her sentence, a loud smash comes from nearby. The fence that divided the soda fountain and Cory's Automotive Service Station falls with a dusty thud.

JQ stands on the other side, power tool and crowbar in hand.

"Who authorized you to do this?" I ask, joking because the last time I hung a sign on the front of the soda fountain he asked me the same question.

"I'll let you two squabble this out. See you this afternoon." Honey waves goodbye.

Hands on hips, I march over, but beam a smile at my man who looks foxy holding those tools.

"I had an idea." JQ outlines his master plan for a patio space for dining, music, and entertainment. "I happen to know a great singer who I'd like to be our debut."

My heart warms over. "And I happen to know someone who recently wrote a new song."

He lights up. "Really?"

"Just in time for our grand opening."

"Hopefully, no more acts of sabotage."

"I don't think we have anything to worry about," JQ says.

"But the person who stuck a rotten fish in the air vent, messed up the soda fountain and the syrup, and caused a major leak is still out there."

JQ winks. "I have a hunch they won't be bothering us anymore."

I can't help but wonder if the cameras he set up provided some answers or at least clues about who didn't want us to reopen the soda fountain.

It's not even nine am and we have a lot of work to do, but we manage to demolish the fence, sweep up the driveway, and cordon off the area for guests later. I hang string lights and decorations, then rescue the old chairs and tables that we replaced with updated items inside the Penny Gamble. I set them around while JQ hooks up a temporary sound system and tells me his vision for evening showcases with pizza on Friday.

I like it. I like it a lot. And I love this man.

After putting the finishing touches on everything, I tell him I'm heading to the apartment to shower.

Fiddling with something by a speaker, JQ says, "Meet me at the back door at a quarter of twelve."

"You got it, boss."

He chuckles at our inside joke.

"And don't forget the rest of those stickers. Peaches will be proud to see herself plastered everywhere."

"Sure thing, boss," he replies.

To make the hate-to-love business partner combo work, we decided to make light of it and discuss everything. When words don't come, we write letters to each other, like Nan and I used to, but they consist of new ideas we might be hesitant the other will veto. Sometimes, there's a P.S. with a request for an extra smooch at the end of the night. And we always call each other boss.

You know, whatever works.

After getting ready for the grand opening at noon—I wear the same sundress as when JQ and I first met. At the precise time he said, I find him at the back of the Penny Gamble with Peaches in tow. She's become our official mascot, one eye and all, with a little cartoon image of her on the T-shirts and other swag we had made to give away today and then sell at the soda fountain.

"Are you ready?" JQ asks, taking a deep breath.

I nod on an exhale. "Are you?"

"Let's take one more spin through before we share it with the rest of Hogwash."

We walk through the back hallway which is largely the same except there's no longer a leak and everything has a fresh coat of paint. We even left Nan's signs, which serve now as a reminder to bring our best even if I'm not the townsfolk's favorite resident since I stole the resident bachelor and supposedly the root beer mug.

We still don't know who the giant crystal root beer mug thief is and it hasn't been recovered. I occasionally get wary looks from Hoggers, like they think I'm guilty and are still fixing to drive me out of town with pitchforks. If I were T. Swizzle, they'd be singing a different tune.

On the other side of the door, JQ and I each take a moment to admire our hard work, the shiny chrome, the polished wood, and the wall covered in an array of old photographs of Hogwash Holler, Nan, Cory, and even a few I found of Hogan Tickle. There is no evidence of the swamp ghosts having wreaked havoc in here. It's an impressive transformation.

"You did good," he says.

"You did too."

We stand on the opposite side of the front door.

"Ready?" JQ asks, gripping my hand tightly.

"It's now or never."

Hand in hand, we open the door, and cross the threshold. A few townsfolk stand on the sidewalk, eyes lifted toward the roof. I take a few steps to find the giant crystal root beer mug slowly rotating.

"Wait. How did that get there? Where did you find it?" When I turn around, I find JQ on one knee, holding a ring pop.

My entire face, no my whole body, tingles. "What? Wait. How?"

He gets to his feet. "I can explain. But first, Lexington,

would you do me the honor of taking me as your husband and being my wife?"

"Yes, I will, Jacques Quill." I wrap my arms around his neck and then we kiss.

Everyone gathered cheers. Maybe they don't hate me after all. When we part, as if we'd planned this—we didn't—we both say, "Welcome to The Penny Gamble and our future."

Tears spring to my eyes because never has anything felt so perfect.

Throughout the afternoon, people come and go, congratulating us on two accounts—the grand opening and our engagement. We serve lots of soda, ice cream, and Sm'ookie squares.

Molly asks if she can get an exclusive interview with us for the Pest Digest. Her sidekick, Roxanne, is nowhere to be seen. However, I do hear murmurings and whispers among Hoggers that the descendants of Hogan Tickle might make a big return to the town. If they're looking for unsolicited advice, they can start by fixing up the Chateau. That place is creep city.

I sense a change in the air or maybe it's just that JQ and I love each other. For the first time in a while, I'm hopeful for the future.

As the sun sets, he leads me outside to the patio where he plans to build a deck for outdoor dining and music. I can kind of see into his backyard and he assures me there will be a new fence, but I'll be on the same side as him.

"So, tell me how you got ahold of the root beer mug," I say.

"Remember, I'm a Navy SEAL."

"You did recce without me?"

"And I cleared your name."

"But who stole it and why?"

"Look for a full confession in the next edition of the Hogwash Holler Township Tattler."

"Is it replacing the Pest Digest?"

"No, now we can claim two gossip rags. Let's just say someone was jealous of you and me. She tried to make you look bad. But it wasn't so much love that was missing from her life, though that's possible. More like something all her own. When she gave me her full confession, I encouraged her to start her own newspaper."

"That sounds like some small-town drama I'd like to stay away from. We'd better get that new fence built real quick...and because I plan to use that pool in your backyard oasis if this heat doesn't let up."

"That'll just be the first of many improvements we're going to invest our treasure in." JQ winks.

We agreed that the gold stays here. We haven't told anyone we found the Golden Token or the treasure but have been quietly investing in Hogwash Holler—new fences for Farmer Daley, sidewalk repairs, fixing the sign to the This & That, and we've been looking for a company to repair the public pool.

The treasure is a secret, but our love isn't. Not anymore.

Leading me by the hand, JQ walks to the center of the patio where there's a microphone and Cory's guitar. He thanks everyone for joining us today and shares a brief backstory about Nan bringing us together.

Someone hoots and someone else hollers about our love connection. I'm guessing it's Honey.

I take to the microphone and say, "Everything he said. Plus, I want to thank y'all for welcoming me to your town, even if I got more than one suspicious side-eye about that root beer mug. I hear a lot of people come here looking for treasure. Well, I found mine, and he's a living, breathing, amazing hero. Someone I'm happy to soon call my husband."

At that, the music pours from me, from my heart, as this hopeful romantic sings and strums the love song I wrote just for us.

Before it's over, JQ gets to the stage, eyes smiling and lips too before he brings them to mine and whispers, "I love you."

"I love you too."

Then Peaches lets loose a howl of happy approval.

Note to readers:

Thank you for reading and spending time in Hogwash Holler with me. I hope you enjoyed the first installment of my new small-town romcom series *On the Hunt for Love*.

While the story is new, longtime readers might spot the Easter Eggs from my other books and series.

I also hope it will pique the curiosity of new readers who might be interested in checking out some of my other books and series. Now that you've read it, it's also available as a paperback.

If you're not ready to leave Hogwash, get the Bitter Heir and the Beauty (Honey and Maddock's fake relationship, secret-filled love story) and continue the scavenger hunt! But be sure to come back and read the author note below!

Here is the breakdown (and if you somehow found yourself here before you read the book, spoiler alert!). Below, I share a quick series summary along with the Easter eggs.

Only Us Series: These billionaires have everything except love... If you like hate-to-love romance, mistaken identities, opposites-attract, off-the-charts chemistry, and a dash of clever suspense, then you'll adore this series.

•Lexi mentions that her friend from college is the Royal Princess of the small, relatively unknown country called Concordia. You'll find this reference specifically in *Only a Night with the Billionaire* as well *Only Love with the Billionaire*.

•Her cowboy cousin also lives there with his wife Charlotte and their kids Birdie, Miriella, Johnny, and their newest addition, Wayne which you'll read about in Only Forever with the Billionaire.

•Concordia is also the setting for the Love List series (see below)

Hawk Ridge Hollow/Hawkins Brothers Series: Looking for an escape into a small town with lots of love, laughter, and happily ever afters? Welcome to Hawk Ridge Hollow. Where the guys are rich and rugged but are missing one thing. True love.

•JQ mentions this small Montana mountain town with a winter sports resort, lots of downtown charm, and an amazing pizza and pie place.

•See the Costas below

• It's the kind of place Hogwash dreams it could be with a

bustling Main Street, thriving businesses, and not a piece of litter in sight.

Blue Bay Beach Reads Series: Fall in love with this summer beach reads clean and wholesome, small-town series with second chance romance, enemies to lovers, and opposites attract love stories.

✔ Flirty & swoony heroes

✔ Strong & sassy heroines

✔ Small town charm

✔ Happily ever afters

Meet your next beach boyfriend in this Hallmark-style, faith-friendly series with heart-warming friendships and love that endures.

•Lexi's friend Cleo lives in Blue Bay Beach with her husband where they have a shop called Cana Market.

•JQ's cousin Tucker, who is a Ritchie and big car buff, lives there with his family. (More on the Ritchies below.)

Ritchie Ranch Cowboys Series: Cowboy hats, moonlight kisses, and small-town charm along with family sagas, romance, and of course, happily ever after. Note: The first three books should be read in order because of a mystery subplot, but the rest stand alone, though reading them in order provides a deeper, richer, and more immersive experience.

•The Ritchies are a notorious Texas family who have a ranch in Smuggler's Springs. JQ's mom is a Ritchie and part of the crew visits their home. Some of them are also accomplished country musicians. One of the bands is called The C.o.w.b.o.y.s.

. . .

Falling into Happily Ever After Series: A sweet, heartwarming & uplifting romantic comedy series, featuring best friends, book boyfriends, one true love, and unforgettable guys

•Lexi's friend Rose runs an ice cream shop called Queen's Cones in Liberty Lake, New Hampshire where she butts heads with public enemy number one, Doug King.

Dare to Love Series: Long ago, a group of friends made a pact. As their high school reunion deadline approaches, they each have to make good on the agreement or else...

Truth? They already know each other's secrets.

Dare? Marry the next guy they each date.

Things are about to get real...messy.

•JQ's Buddy Shaw was an associate in military intelligence. He's also the original Boy Scout and he and Cora have to survive the jungles of the Amazon in the first installment of this series.

Home Sweet Home Series: Four women compete to land the coveted Mrs. Fix-It role on the famed home improvement show, opposite the hammer-wielding stud, Mr. Fix-It. After a series of comedic mishaps, they go into business together buying, remodeling, and fixing up homes, landing them with their own show, Designed to Last. As they build their own happily ever afters, they also discover a strange mystery in Butterbury and have to solve it to save the quaint, small town from underwater ruin.

•Everly, Lexi's friend, mentions the Designed to Last ladies who may or may not have a hand in helping makeover Hogwash Holler.

. . .

The Costa Brothers Cozy Christmas Comfort Romance Series: Meet the Costa family. A bit loud. A little crazy. A whole lotta lovable! These six brothers go all in, opening a pizza parlor in a small town to help out their retired parents. They anticipate success, but they're not expecting to find love. This clean, feel-good, romantic comedy series brings laughs, friends to love, enemies to love, second chances, grumpy guys, cinnamon rolls, and a lot of sunshine despite the backdrop of winter!

•JQ mentions how he and Cory once went skiing in a little town in Montana called Hawk Ridge Hollow (see above). They have the best pizza and pie shop called *Costa's Pizza and Pie*, which inspired JQ's pizza oven.

The Love List Series: Five bad boy football players get into trouble after a prank goes wrong and are sent to reform school. Read this clean romantic comedy series where jocks become gentlemen, women get treated like royalty, and all the sass and spark in between.

•Everly and her edible cookie dough feature in this series. She lives on an island in Michigan with the love of her life and a former NFL star.

•Lexi wears a Boston Bruisers hat. JQ prefers the Golden Sons, the Louisiana team. For the record, the Bruisers are the superior team, despite their hijinks. Oh, and Dustin Bruber is not real.

Love, Laughs, and Mystery in Coco Key Series: Four brothers, a falling out, a family fortune, and an island. Lost treasure and found love. Plus the secret sister in this romantic comedy series where Schitts Creek meets Virgin River but on an island + the mystery and thrills of Lost City with Sandra Bullock and Channing Tatum.

•As the scavenger hunt in Hogwash Holler intensifies, look for some crossover between these two series!

Look for the next book in *On the Hunt for Love* series and a hockey romcom series called *Nebraska Knights Holiday Hockey Romance*.

THE HOGWASH HOLLER TOWNSHIP TATTLER

WELCOME TO THE NEWEST PUBLICATION FOR ALL OUR HOGGERS HERE IN TOWN WHO WANT TO LEARN MORE ABOUT OUR HISTORY, CURRENT EVENTS, AND THOSE OF YOU INTERESTED IN THE FIBER ARTS, KNITTING SPECIFICALLY. THE LATEST EDITION WILL BE AVAILABLE AT THE THIS & THAT ON FRIDAYS, JUST IN TIME FOR YOUR WEEKEND PERUSAL. AND WITHOUT FURTHER ADO, ONTO OUR LATEST STORIES.

The mystery of the crystal root beer mug has been solved. One of our very own Hoggers put his sleuthing skills to work and discovered the world's largest rotating root beer mug in an abandoned box truck parked on Coronet's farm.

Records show the property owner recently contacted authorities regarding an unusual commotion that sounded like someone screaming but turned out to be a goat that got loose. However, there was no evidence that he spotted or reported the recently deserted vehicle.

Retired Navy SEAL, town mechanic, and previously single local loner was scouting the area, discovered the truck, and offered the farmer two new tires and a rebalance on his Chevrolet in exchange for the vehicle and its contents.

When asked for comment, he gave none. However, that old Chevy farm truck is back up and running if you startle awake at the sound of a loud muffler at five am.

Supposedly, the rotating root beer mug was packed in the rear of the box truck. Sources aren't certain whether it was for storage and safekeeping or in the process of being stolen.

Although we don't typically outright name names in the Tattler, one Roxanne Lagniappe came forward once the search for the mug was recovered and returned to its owner. She submitted a public apology exclusive to the Tattler.

To root beer drinkers everywhere, I am very sorry that any actions I may or may not have taken interfered with your enjoyment of the official Hogwash town beverage. There was a misunderstanding about the relocation of the mug and like everyone, I am glad to have it back in safe hands. In case anyone is wondering, the key isn't there.

Yours most sincerely,
Roxy, founder of the Tattler

P.S. Turn the page for our latest knitting pattern available for sale at Etsbay.com

P.S. That last part sounds like code, but we're not here to ask questions. Rather, we give answers and let you do the rest.

About the Author

Ellie Hall is a USA Today bestselling author. If only that meant she could wear a tiara and get away with it ;) She loves puppies, books, and the ocean. Writing sweet romance with lots of firsts and fizzy feels brings her joy. Oh, and chocolate chip cookies are her fave.
Ellie believes in dreaming big, working hard, and lazy Sunday afternoons spent with her family and dog in gratitude for God's grace.

Let's Connect

Do you love sweet, swoony romance?
Stories with happy endings?
Falling in love?

Please subscribe to my newsletter to receive updates about my latest books, exclusive extras, deals, and other fun and sparkly things, including a FREE eBook, the *The Secret Book Boyfriend*!

Get your free copy here: www.elliehall.com 🤍

Also by Ellie Hall

All books are clean and wholesome, Christian faith-friendly and without mature content but filled with swoony kisses and happily ever afters. Books are listed under series in recommended reading order.

-select titles available in audiobook, paperback, hardcover, and large print-

The Only Us Sweet Billionaire Series

Only a Date with a Billionaire

Only a Kiss with a Billionaire

Only a Night with a Billionaire

Only Forever with a Billionaire

Only Love with a Billionaire

Only Christmas with a Billionaire

Only New Year with a Billionaire

The Only Us Sweet Billionaire series box set (books 2-5) + a bonus scene!

Hawkins Family Small Town Romance Series

Second Chance in Hawk Ridge Hollow

Finding Forever in Hawk Ridge Hollow

Coming Home to Hawk Ridge Hollow

Falling in Love in Hawk Ridge Hollow

Christmas in Hawk Ridge Hollow

The Hawk Ridge Hollow Series Complete Collection Box Set (books 1-5)

The Blue Bay Beach Reads Romance Series

Summer with a Marine

Summer with a Rock Star

Summer with a Billionaire

Summer with the Cowboy

Summer with the Carpenter

Summer with the Doctor

Books 1-3 Box Set

Books 4-6 Box Set

Ritchie Ranch Clean Cowboy Romance Series

Rustling the Cowboy's Heart (Book 1)

Lassoing the Cowboy's Heart (Book 2)

Trusting the Cowboy's Heart (Book 3)

Kissing the Christmas Cowboy

Loving the Cowboy's Heart

Wrangling the Cowboy's Heart

Charming the Cowboy's Heart

Saving the Cowboy's Heart

Ritchie Ranch Romance Books 1-4 Box Set

Falling into Happily Ever After Rom Com

An Unwanted Love Story

An Unexpected Love Story

An Unlikely Love Story

An Accidental Love Story

An Impossible Love Story

An Unconventional Christmas Love Story

Forever Marriage Match Romantic Comedy Series

Dare to Love My Grumpy Boss

Dare to Love the Guy Next Door

Dare to Love My Fake Husband

Dare to Love the Guy I Hate

Dare to Love My Best Friend

Home Sweet Home Series

Mr. and Mrs. Fix It Find Love

Designing Happily Ever After

The DIY Kissing Project

The True Romance Renovation: Christmas Edition

Extreme Heart Makeover

Building What's Meant to Be

The Costa Brothers Cozy Christmas Comfort Romance Series

Tommy & Merry and the 12 Days of Christmas

Bruno & Gloria and the 5 Golden Rings

Luca & Ivy and the 4 Calling Birds

Gio & Joy and the 3 French Hens

Paulo & Noella and the 2 Turtle Doves

Nico & Hope and the Partridge in the Pear Tree

The Love List Series

The Swoon List

The Not Love List

The Crush List

The Kiss List

The Naughty or Nice List

Love, Laughs & Mystery in Coco Key

Clean romantic comedy, family secrets, and treasure *These books should be read in the following order:

The Romance Situation

The Romance Fiasco

The Romance Game

The Romance Gambit

The Christmas Romance Wish

The Nebraska Knights Holiday Hockey Romance Series

Stupid Cupid

Redd, Whit & Blue

The Kiss Class

Margo & the Faux Good Luck Beau

The Ex-Puck Bunny

Love at First Skate (Tie-In)

Love in Hockey Town (Ties in to the Nebraska Knights)

His Jersey

My Wife

Her Goal

On the Hunt for Love

Sweet, Small Town & Southern

The Grump & the Girl Next Door

The Bitter Heir & the Beauty

The Secret Son & the Sweetheart

The Ex-Best Friend & the Fake Fiancee

The Best Friend's Brother & the Brain

Don't You Forget About Tea (Tie-In)

SoCal Summer Kisses

We Go Together

The One I Want

Hopelessly Devoted

Stand Alone Titles

Happily Ever Haunted (a romcom - ghost mashup)

The Secret Book Boyfriend (small town, grumpy sunshine)

Madeleine's Mistletoe Meet Cute (small town, mistaken identity)

Visit www.elliehallauthor.com or your favorite retailer for more.

If you love my books, please leave a review on your favorite retailer's website! Thank you! 🖤 Ellie

P.S. I have a clean fantasy and paranormal romance pen name: E. Hall that you might enjoy (best read in listed order):

The Court of Crown and Compass Series

Fae of Light and Shadow (prequel)

Fae of the North (book 1)

Fae of the West (book 2)

Fae of the South (book 3)

Fae of the East (book 4)

RIP Magic Academy Reform School Series

Law & Disorder (book 1)

Crime & Curses (book 2)

Mayhem & Magic (book 3)

Shifter Diaries

Life Fated (book 1)

Lies Tamed (book 2)

Loss Hunted (book 3)

Love United (book 4)

Made in United States
North Haven, CT
12 July 2025

70623208R00106